Slayer In A Gray Toupee

AXEL HATCHETT MYSTERY VOL. 3

Steven LeRoy Nelson

BLOOD AND THUNDER PRESS

BLOOD AND THUNDER PRESS
3612 Sheffield Lane
Colorado Springs, CO 80907
www.bloodandthunderpress.com

ISBN: 1940469015
ISBN-13: 978-1-940469-01-0

To my little cabbage roll.

1

I met the old couple in their home. Dunston and Cleo Flinders were homebodies, and right now, they were not merely unwilling to go out, they were afraid to. Dunston — Dunty to his friends and family — had received a death threat in the mail only a few days before. And then, this morning, a strange package.

"Of course we called the police," Cleo assured me. "But they weren't able to do anything last time so we don't have much confidence in them."

"Last time?" I asked.

The old man cleared his throat. "I'm not sure how much Mayhew told you on the phone."

Mayhew was the family butler. He'd called me that morning and arranged for me to come talk to his employers about a murder threat, but he hadn't given me any details.

"He told me damned little," I said. "You've received other death threats in the past?"

"Not me. My brother. The late Waldrous Flinders. He was murdered, horribly, in this very house. Six months ago."

"Seven," Cleo butted in.

"Six and a half. Someone sent him a series of letters, telling him that he would soon die. And then, the package. Very like the gift I received by post this morning."

"I'd hardly call it a gift," snorted Cleo.

"Well, for lack of a better word — "

"What was in the package?" I asked. I sipped my tea from a frail china cup. I don't really like tea, but it's what they'd offered me, and it was cold and snowing outside.

"A gray toupee." Said Dunty. "Sounds like a joke, doesn't it?"

"It's certainly strange. You say your brother also got a gray toupee in the mail? Or was it a different color?"

"Gray. A very nice one. The police took it. They still have it."

"That's the cops for you. Always taking folks' stuff and never returning it. Do gray toupees have any particular significance for you?"

"Of course not. Not for me. But my brother reacted with great fear when he unwrapped his package and discovered what it was. However, he refused to talk about it. Right up to the end, he kept mum."

There was something peculiarly English about this old couple, though I was sure that at least Dunty had been born and raised right here in

Quartz Quarry, Colorado. Maybe he'd been educated in Britain, I didn't know. What I did know was that he was the son of Benji "Flinty" Flinders, a dirt poor, hard-scrabble miner who had come west to join the forty-niners in California. He intended to strike it rich in California, but he'd stopped in Colorado first and had struck pay dirt in our own humble gold fields. He was filthy rich in no time. He'd built the rambling granite mansion whose great room I was presently sitting in.

"How was your brother killed?"

Dunty cleared his throat again. "A knife. A large kukri. Are you familiar with that type of knife?"

"I think so. The Gurkhas use them in India."

"Correct. Waldrous and I always had an interest in exotic and primitive weapons. I have quite a trophy room full of them."

"Oh? And did the murder weapon come from this trophy room?"

"No. the killer brought his own. He came in through my brother's bedroom window, even though there was a bodyguard on duty, and cut the poor fellows head clean off."

"Don't be brutal," said Cleo.

"That's how it happened. This detective needs to know how things happened."

"True enough," I said. "Your brother never revealed to you, or anyone, why someone would want to murder him, or what the gray toupee meant to him?"

"No. It is still a mystery."

The old couple looked like something out of the nineteenth century, right down to their clothes. Dunty, a shock of white hair sprinkled with red sprouting above his liver-spotted forehead, wore an old-fashioned velvet jacket with frogs around the button holes. I think they're called frogs. The way Cleo rustled every time she moved, she must have been wearing starched petticoats under her gray satin dress. Her luxuriant hair was black, but she wasn't the first owner.

The great room we were in was just as outdated, with its antique furniture and the roaring fire in the ornate stone fireplace. I felt like it was 1856 instead of 1956.

"The police did nothing," said Cleo. "Nothing. I hope you'll be more efficient and useful, Mr. — ?"

"Hatchett. Axel Hatchett. Call me Axe. I'll do everything I can, Mrs. Flinders. I won't let your husband be murdered. But I would suggest he hire some type of bodyguard."

"Already been done, sir," Said Dunty. "Dirk Drebber is on the job. He was Waldrous' bodyguard, and I rehired him as soon as I received the first threat."

"Maybe you should have hired someone else."

"No. It was not Dirk's fault that my brother was killed. The killer shot Dirk in the neck, through a broken pane in the window, with a dart from a blow gun. The dart was poisoned. It temporarily paralyzed Dirk. By the time he recovered, Waldrous' head had been severed from his neck."

"Don't be coarse, Dunty," said Cleo.

"The fellow needs to know how things were, Cleo. Anyway, Dirk will keep his eye out for poisoned darts this time."

"Sure, I'm always watching out for poisoned darts myself, and unexpected boomerangs. Are you taking any other precautions?"

"Well, as we've said, we contacted the police."

"I'm sure they won't do anything," said Cleo. "Useless lot."

"I'm sure they'll do what they can," I said. "In the meantime, is there anyone either of you can think of who might want Mr. Flinders dead?"

"Of course not," said Cleo. "Everyone loves my husband."

"Hardly everyone, dear. I may have made some enemies during my business dealings. Such things happen. But I can't think of anyone specifically. As for my personal life, I seem to get along with people pretty well."

"He spoils the servants dreadfully."

"I treat them as they ought to be treated. Like devoted and loyal family pets."

"How many servants are there in the household?" I asked.

"Seven," said Dunty, "though only six of them actually live in the mansion. Cam, the chauffeur and gardener, lives in the carriage house."

"How long have these folks been employed by you?"

"Well, Mayhew, our butler, has been with us for thirty years. Abigail, the cook, has been here almost as long. Simone, the housekeeper, has been here five years. Bosco, the court jester, has been with us for seven years."

"Eight," said Cleo.

"You employ a court jester?" I asked. "I've been meaning to get one of those for the office. Can you recommend a good talent agency?"

"Not really. It was Cleo's idea," said Dunty.

"We don't get out much," she explained. "We choose not to. And we can't abide television. We find it quite common. We hired Bosco to entertain us, and he does a splendid job."

"I'm a bit tired of the fellow myself," said Dunty.

"Yes, but you haven't a very developed sense of humor."

"OK," I said, "you've named five servants. Who are the other two?"

"The maids, Mavis and Mary Elizabeth."

"And how long have they been with you?"

"Let me answer," Cleo told Dunty. "I'll get it right. Mavis, the older of the two, has been in our employ four years. Mary Elizabeth was brought on three years ago."

"I think it was two," said Dunty.

"Almost three."

"So all of the servants were working here at the time of Waldrous Flinders' murder?"

"Yes," said Dunty. "We had a hard time keeping some of them here after the tragic event. Can't blame them, really."

I spoke to Dunty. "Any reason to believe any of the help would want you dead?"

"No. I think they are all rather attached to me."

Cleo broke in. "Surely the servants aren't suspects? The killer is at large somewhere. The person who killed Waldrous is the same as the one who has threatened Dunty. Some outsider."

"Maybe," I said, "But we don't know that. It could be that whoever has threatened your husband may be using the murder as a cover-up, a way of putting suspicion on someone else. Are you with me?"

"Nonsense. We don't employ that type of servant," said Cleo.

"How well can you possibly know them? They have private lives just like you. By the way, you didn't tell me how long this Cam, the chauffeur, has been with you."

"Seventeen years," said Dunty. He turned to his wife. "Don't argue, my dear."

"Why would I? Yes, Cam has been with us for seventeen years."

"You guys must be easy to work for."

"I should think so," said Cleo, puffing up like a pouter pigeon.

"Listen," I said, "I'll need to talk to all these servants."

"The police already did so," said Cleo.

"That's fine, but I don't know what the cops

found out. I'll need to question the servants myself. I don't suppose they'll like it, but I'm sure they'll understand that it's necessary. Is anyone else staying in the house with you?"

"Yes," said Dunty, "my biographer. My cousin Larkspur's nephew, Paddy Cotton. He's been with us some months. He was also here at the time of my brother's death. And he has a secretary, a Miss Ursula Camille. I suppose you want to question them as well?"

"I do."

"You'll have plenty of time for that. You'll be staying with us until the would-be murderer is apprehended."

"What? You want me to stay here? I'm not sure about that. I'll likely have plenty of leg work to do. I'll need to work out of my office."

"I don't see why," said Cleo. "We can set up some sort of office for you here. Besides, it's not negotiable. We've already made up our minds. Dirk will be guarding Dunty by day and sleeping on a cot in Dunty's room during the night. You will sleep during the day so that you can guard the house at night. Is that clear?"

"If I'd known that's what you had in mind I would have packed a suitcase."

"You can certainly return to your home and pack your things and return here. That shouldn't take long."

"I'm to be a prisoner in your house?" I could feel my neck swelling around my collar.

"Of course not. You'll have as much freedom as any of the servants. Take it or leave it. I believe there are other detectives for hire in Quartz Quarry."

"Cleo and I have made up our minds," said Dunty. "You'll be well taken care of. A spacious and comfortable bedroom, and Abigail's fine cooking. If you need clothes laundered or pressed, the housekeeper, Simone, will see to it."

I thought about it. I didn't like it, but I needed the work. "OK. I'll stay until the person making the threats is caught."

"Excellent," said Dunty. "Good for you, old boy."

Old boy indeed. I was a good forty-five years younger than either one of these aged birds.

Cleo bestowed a smile on me. Her teeth were as white, and as obviously false, as the cotton beard of a department-store Santa. Speaking of Santa Claus, when I glanced out the huge latticed window nearest me, I saw the snow was now coming down in fat, fluffy flakes. It looked like they were having a big pillow fight in Heaven and it'd gotten out of hand. I'd parked my Nash on a side street near the estate. I hoped no hasty motorist would slide into it because of the snow.

"This chauffeur of yours, you say he lives in the carriage house. Would he be there now?"

"I imagine," said Dunty. "He might be out plowing snow. I'll have Mayhew ring him up and see."

"Thanks," I said. "I might as well talk to him first. Where is the carriage house exactly?"

"If you step out the front door," said Dunty, "and follow the stone path, you'll reach it in about ten minutes time. Do you mind the walk, or would you have us summon Cam to the mansion?"

"I'll walk down there myself, by all means."

"We can have Bosco accompany you to prevent you from getting lost or stranded."

"I'm sure that's not necessary."

"Try to be back by dinner time," said Cleo. "We dine at six. A bit early, but Dunty and I retire to bed earlier than when we were younger."

I heard a noise outside, the sound of a truck engine perhaps, and a scraping sound. I looked out the window in time to see a tractor, pulling some kind of makeshift snowplow, make a U-turn in front of the paved entry as it headed back the way it had apparently come. It was swallowed up by the storm almost at once.

"That would be Cam," said Dunty. "If you hurry, you might catch him and ask him to come inside."

"No, let the poor guy get back to his fire and warm his toes in peace before I give him the third degree."

"If that's what you wish." Dunty reached for a bell — the kind that old-time school marms used to wield — and gave it a good shake. In no more than a minute a tall, stout, bald old man made his stately entrance. He was dressed in a suit of very nice gray flannel and he exuded calm efficiency .

"Mayhew," said Dunty, "Cam is plowing the walkways. Give him half an hour to return home and then ring him up. Tell him that a Mr. Hatchett, a detective in our employ, would like to have a word with him. The detective will meet him at the carriage house. Impress on Cam the importance of his cooperation."

"Very good, sir." Mayhew bowed very slightly to all of us and disappeared as gracefully as he had appeared.

2

I spent the next half hour talking with the Flinders, drinking more tea, and consuming a series of little cakes and pastries apparently prepared by Abigail, their cook. If this was any example of her cooking skills, I wouldn't mind staying here at all.

When the thirty minutes had passed, Mayhew returned to the great room and informed his master that Cam was at home and was ready to receive me. I don't know why he didn't just tell me; I was sitting right there. Something to do with butler etiquette no doubt. I climbed into my overcoat, pulled my fedora on tight enough to keep it from blowing off in the wind, and got ready to brave the storm. Mayhew opened the front door for me and wished me a safe journey.

Once outside I could hardly see ten feet in front of me, and the snow was already obliterating the wide stone walk that Cam had so recently plowed. I turned up the collar of my coat, leaned into the wind I was facing, and made my hesitant way in the direction of the carriage house. It took me twenty minutes, not ten, to walk the distance between the mansion and the stone, barn-like, structure where Cam was.

The snow was so thick I didn't even catch a glimpse of the place until I was no more than ten yards from it. Yellow light showed in a couple of windows, one downstairs and one upstairs where the living quarters must be. I rapped my knuckles hard against the big oak front door, wondering if anyone inside would be able to hear me. I kept this up for about five minutes before the door finally creaked open on frosty hinges.

A short but sturdily-built man looked out at me and then hastened me inside. I found myself in a big room with a glowing wood stove and a couple of oil lamps lit on a long table that looked more like a workbench. Cam motioned me to a wing chair with worn upholstery and took my hat and coat, shaking the snow off of them for me. On one side of the room were two cars. One a flashy yellow Rolls Royce about the length of a Pullman car, the other an ordinary Buick station wagon. I introduced myself.

"Would you like some coffee?" asked Cam.

"I'll say. Make it nice and hot, will you? I take it black."

He took a big speckled coffee pot off of the stove and filled a crockery mug on the table. He handed it to me and I drank it right down, steaming as it was.

"I guess the butler told you why I'm here," I said.

Cam sat down in a chair that was the twin to mine. "Yeah. The old man wants I should talk to you. I already talked to the cops."

"I know, but I haven't talked to them, and they wouldn't have anything to say to me if I did. I hate to make you repeat yourself, but that's the way it's going to be. I'll pump you as little as I have to."

"Sure. I guess that's OK, you coming down here through the snow and all, I wouldn't want you should go away with nothing."

"Not to mention the fact that Mr. Flinders made it clear you should cooperate with me."

"He's a softy. He wouldn't ride me much if I didn't tell you what you want. But I'm going to, see?"

"Let's get started. You've been with the Flinders family for seventeen years. Easy job?"

He shrugged. "Lots of work, but I don't mind. Pay ain't bad, and the old folks leave me alone. I keep busy, but I do what I want. I try to stay outside when I can. I don't like being cooped up, like today. I only been out once to scoop snow."

"Do you have a key to the mansion?"

"Of course not. The housekeeper has all the keys. Maybe Mayhew's got some keys, too. I don't know. Why?"

"Just a question. Do you know any members of the household staff who might benefit if Mr. Flinders died?"

"All of us. He's leaving us money. The longer we been working here, the more we'll get. I could be fixed when he pops off, but I don't know. He talks about the trusts he's set up for us, but he doesn't mention how much he's leaving anybody."

"I see. Any member of the staff, that you know of, who might especially need money right now?"

"No. Bosco wants money so he can buy his own bar, but he can wait. Everybody else is doing all right, as far as I know. Those folks don't talk to me. Kind of snooty. Just because I live out here instead of in the big house, I guess. Besides, I like to keep to myself."

"How about bad blood between Mr. Flinders and one of the servants?"

"Naw. Are you kidding? He treats us right. You couldn't hate the guy if you wanted to. Really, we'll all miss him when he's gone. The missus, she ain't as easy to get along with. Too bad the old man's got a bad ticker. He could go any day."

"Flinders has a bad heart?"

"That's the story. He even takes — what is it? Something like dynamite."

"Nitroglycerin?"

"That's it. Any more questions?"

"A couple. What do you know about this Paddy character and his little secretary?"

"The secretary, Ursula, she's a looker. Won't give me the time of day, even though I haven't made any moves on her or nothing. That Cotton guy, he's something. A regular piccolo"

"You mean gigolo? Is that Paddy's last name, Cotton?"

"Yeah. He's writing some book about the old man. So he says. All I've ever heard he does is chase skirts."

"Would you happen to know if he'll inherit money when Mr. Flinders dies?"

"Couldn't tell you. I keep to myself. Or try to."

There was a lull in the storm. The wind died down and I heard boards creaking upstairs.

"You married?" I asked.

"No. You?"

"Not yet. You live with someone?"

"No. That noise you heard just now, that's squirrels. They gnaw their way through the roof and into the attic. Then they gnaw their way into the rooms. I'd put out traps, but the old man would throw a fit. Like I said, he's a softy."

"Sounds like quite a problem, those squirrels, considering the noise they're making What do you feed them, iron filings and old horseshoes? Listen, thanks for your time. I don't think I have any more questions for you right now."

"You going back out in that snow? You want I should take you on the tractor? There's only one seat, but you could sit on my lap."

"I'll walk, thanks." I got up to go. The upstairs boards creaked again. Cam didn't look up, but kept his eyes on my face. "I gather you don't take your meals at the mansion."

"No. I do my own cooking. Sometimes Mayhew brings me leftovers. I make out OK."

I pulled my coat and hat back on. I opened the front door and was blasted by wind-blown snow. The storm was picking up again, and it was getting dark.

I should have taken the offered tractor ride, though I really hadn't wanted to sit on Cam's lap. The recently-plowed walkway already had a couple of inches of new snow on it. I couldn't see five feet in front of me, and the wind blew me from behind like I weighed nothing. I wished I'd brought a flashlight, or borrowed one from the chauffeur.

I struggled against the whipping snowflakes and tried to keep from straying off the path. What a way to die. I wondered if the Flinders would send Bosco the jester out to find me if I didn't show up after a couple of hours.

Finally the lights of the house came into sight, but the closer I got, the more I felt there was something wrong with those lights. There weren't as many, for one thing. And they weren't steady. It could be the snow was making them look like they were flickering, but I didn't think so.

Then I figured it out. The storm had knocked out the electricity. What I was looking at was light from candles, maybe oil lamps, like at Cam's, only I'd gotten the impression the carriage house wasn't wired for electricity, at least not the downstairs. Having the power off could make things interesting. Whoever the would-be killer was, he'd have a better opportunity with the lights out. I wondered if the phone lines were down, too. If they were, then I couldn't call Tracy, my girl-friend, and she'd wonder what the hell had happened to me. But she was a smart girl, she'd figure things out.

I was no more than a few yards from the front door when it opened and two figures stepped out. One was carrying what looked like a kerosene lantern. The other one was tapping at the walkway with a cane like he was blind. They were both so bundled up I could only guess they were men and not women. We shouted at each other at about the same time. Then I put on more steam and came into the warm glow of their flickering lantern. All three of us went through the broad front doors and inside.

"We were terribly concerned about you, sir." It was Mayhew. He was unwinding a long woolen scarf and pulling a stocking cap off of his bald head. His heavy winter coat made him look huge, especially since the guy with him was pint sized. We got out of our wraps and Mayhew shook off the snow and hung everything on a hall tree bris-tling with hooks.

Now that I had a good look at the little guy, I couldn't believe it. He was dressed up in tights, a parti-colored tunic, and goofy shoes that turned up at the ends. There were bells sewn all over his costume. I was wondering where the funny hat was when he picked it up off a hall table and put it on. An honest-to-God court jester.

"I hope you aren't horribly chilled, sir," said Mayhew. "We were hoping Cam would drive you back to the house."

"He offered me a ride on the tractor, but I didn't want to sit on his lap."

"My word, sir, why wouldn't he have brought you back in the Buick?"

"You mean that flagged path is wide enough for a car?"

"Certainly, even for the Rolls. He often drives right up to the door to pick up Mr. and Mrs. Flinders."

"Interesting."

"Well, at least you seem to be all right. Dinner is about to be served. Did you want me to show you to your room so you can change?"

"I don't have any clothes with me besides what I'm wearing. By the way, you better get some faucets started dripping or the pipes might freeze."

"That has already been taken care of, sir. Shall I lead you straight to the dining room?"

"Wait. Are your phones still working?"

"Yes, sir. I rang up Cam only a few minutes ago."

"Great. Can I borrow one of them for a moment?"

"Certainly, sir. You'll want to use the one in Mr. Flinders' office. For privacy."

He led me out of the front hall and down a corridor to a large office furnished with a huge walnut desk and matching bookcases. The phone was on the desk. Mayhew closed the door behind him after leaving me to myself, and I called up Tracy at Rocko's.

"Yeah, Rocko's," a screechy voice answered. My beloved.

"Listen, my little horseradish bud, it's Axe. I'm on a case over at the Flinders' mansion."

"Lucky you. If you see any money or gold bars laying around, bring them to Mama, will you?"

"I'll keep my eyes peeled. I'm working an inside death-threat job. The electricity just went off over here. There's a lot of big trees around the house. I expect the phone lines to get knocked down at some point. I just wanted you to know where I am and what's up."

"Thanks, dumpling. Stay away from the chamber maids, OK?"

"Sure. I'll look the other way every time one passes by."

We rang off and I stepped out into the hall. Mayhew was waiting for me.

"This way, sir. I'll show you to the dining room."

We went back down the hall and passed through the great room. The dining room was through a large double doorway. There were plenty of candles lighting up the place. A long table with some nice linen and even nicer china and silver took up its fair share of space. Dunty and Cleo were seated at each end, easily within shouting distance. The ridiculous Bosco sat at Cleo's elbow in a giant high chair.

There were three other diners besides myself. A silver-haired guy around fifty who looked like he ought to be a movie star, a divine blonde dish sitting next to him, who was being very attentive to Silver Hair, and across from them was a big shapeless guy, around forty-something, with a gray crew-cut and a red drinker's nose.

Mayhew pulled out a chair for me right beside this guy. Cleo made introductions.

"Mr. Hatchett, I would like you to meet your fellow diners. To my right here is Bosco, who I believe you've already met. Across from you is Mr. Cotton, Paddy, our relation and Dunty's biographer. Next to him is Ursula, his able secretary. Finally, the gentleman on your left is Dirk, Dunty's bodyguard. Ladies and gentlemen, this is Mr. Axel Hatchett, a detective in our employ."

We all murmured our hellos. A couple of young women, wearing black dresses, frilly white aprons, and tiny white hats, came into the room carrying dishes of very fragrant food. They kept making trips back to the kitchen until our table was overladen with steaming edibles.

I didn't recognize every dish, but my taste buds appreciated them all. I wondered why everyone in the house didn't weigh at least a couple-hundred pounds. But only Dunty and the big sap next to me, Dirk, were overweight.

The maids were swell. The oldest, maybe thirty, had a severe but pretty face, a round figure, and a lot of light brown hair twisted and pinned up to fit under her cap. The other maid couldn't have been more than twenty-one or twenty-two, if that, and had golden-blond hair that gleamed in the candle-light. She was damned close to beautiful, but her looks were a little spoiled by a pouty expression. She was slimmer than her coworker, but still nicely curved.

After they'd finished hauling in the food, the maids hung around to help us eat. I got the impression they would have cut up our meat for us if we'd asked, or pounded us on the back if we'd shown indications of choking. However, I discovered I was able to eat my entire meal without anybody's assistance.

"Mr. Hatchett?"

"Yes, Mrs. Flinders."

"These are our two maids. Mavis and Mary Elizabeth." Cleo gestured toward the younger one. "We call her The Princess." She smiled in a simpering way. "I know you'll be wanting to talk to them both after dinner."

"Yes, if I may."

The only bad thing about the meal was that damned Bosco. He wouldn't keep his mouth shut. He told joke after joke, and they were mostly bad. I recognized a lot of the jokes from recent TV shows — Jack Benny and George Burns — and some of them I recalled from my childhood.

"Did you hear the one about the Jewish doctor who performed circumcisions?" Bosco asked us. "Some Jew asks him what he charges. The Doc says, 'Nothing, I only take tips.' Get it? He only takes tips!"

"That's horribly risqué, Bosco," said Cleo, but she laughed like a loon. In fact, she laughed at every one of his lame jokes. The only other person who laughed was Bosco.

"I just flew in from New York today," he stated. "Boy, are my arms tired!"

Cleo had fits over that one.

"Mavis!" said Bosco, "What was that dirty look you just gave me? I'm wounded. But it's only a flesh wound. The fleshy part of the heart!"

Cleo almost choked on her mirth.

I couldn't wait for dessert. I didn't care what we were having, I just knew it would mark the end of the meal and the end of Bosco's humorless jokes. We were served some kind of banana flambé something-or-other, which we consumed, and were then free to go.

Dunty suggested that the gentlemen should retire to the library for cigars and brandy. I'm not much of a brandy man, but I'll take a good cigar any day, and I figured Dunty could afford good ones. I wasn't wrong; he passed out Cubans from a big mahogany humidor. I'm sure the brandy was extra special too.

3

The library was an unnecessarily-large room filled with enough books to last an army a year. There was a hi-fi playing some kind of longhair, Classical music, and comfortable chairs and couches were spread around. I had coffee with my cigar and mostly listened to Dunty and Paddy talk to each other. Bosco had gone off with Cleo to tell her more of his stale jokes, but the secretary, Ursula, joined the gentlemen. She didn't smoke any cigars, but she had her fair share of brandy, and took dictation, I swear, while the two relatives talked.

They started out talking about some harrowing incident regarding Dunty's adolescence, but pretty soon they were discussing the old man's recent business ventures.

"What a great idea," Paddy told Dunty at one point. "What imagination! No wonder you've doubled the Flinders' fortune."

"Oh, I've hardly done that."

"Did you hear, Axe?" Paddy turned to me. Somehow, we were already on a first name basis. "Dunty's breeding miniature buffalo to be sold as household pets. Brilliant." He turned back to Dunty. "Can I make a suggestion? How would it be if you trimmed those baby bison up like poodles? Huh? What do you think?"

"Excellent notion. Yes. They resemble poodles in appearance somewhat."

Paddy turned back to me. "Axe, would you like to hear about Dunty's absolutely best business investment?"

"Sure. Shoot."

"Wrap your mind around this. Dunty's working on a special kind of sheep fodder. Know what it does?"

"Makes them fat?"

"No, better than that. It makes them grow different colors of wool. Even variegated. Think of the money he'll save not having to dye the wool in dying vats."

"Could make him another fortune," I said, but without much enthusiasm.

"I'll say. It's even better than his sugar beet idea."

"What idea is that?" I asked, though I really didn't want to know.

"He's developing a type of sugar beet that tastes exactly like maple syrup."

"Well, I'm not quite there yet," Dunty demurred.

"Close! Close! It'll happen," gushed Paddy.

We were interrupted at this point by Mayhew's entrance. He stood quietly by his master's chair until there was a lull in the conversation.

"Yes, Mayhew?" asked Dunty.

"Sir. Considering the present temperature outdoors, combined with our temporary lack of central heating — "

"Yes?"

"Would it be wise, sir, if Bosco and I aired out the private crypts?"

"Do you really think the pipes will burst?"

"Perhaps. It's best to be prepared. Bosco and I have brought up a couple of empty wine casks from the cellar and filled them with water in case of such an emergency."

"Quick thinking, Mayhew. Yes, by all means, air out the private crypts. But surely you should wait until the weather has become at least marginally less inclement. I wouldn't want either you or Bosco to freeze."

"No time like the present. We will wrap up well, sir."

"Yes. And Mayhew?"

"Sir?"

"Are there any more empty wine barrels down cellar?"

"No sir."

"Well, perhaps you could fill the bathtubs in all the guest rooms. If the water pipes freeze we'll need plenty of water for cooking and for washing up."

"Excellent idea, sir. I'll see to it as soon as we've aired out the private crypts."

"Have you checked to make sure all the fireplaces are in working order?"

"Yes, sir. And we've put a supply of firewood in each room."

"Good fellow."

"Will that be all, sir?"

"I believe so. Thank you, Mayhew."

"A privilege, sir."

Mayhew bowed and left. Before Dunty and Paddy resumed their discussion of Dunty's business dealings, I stepped in with a couple of questions.

"Excuse me, Mr. Flinders."

"Yes?"

"What's all this talk about private crypts? Are you expecting some of us to freeze to death?"

He chuckled, somewhat self-consciously.

"Well, actually, that's something of a euphemism. A joke, I suppose. About twenty years ago we experienced considerable difficulties with our indoor plumbing. In fact, many of our water and sewer pipes had to be replaced. In the meantime, it was considered expedient to erect a couple of — shall we say — outdoor lavatories. Privies, if you will. I was concerned with their aesthetic appearance as well as their functionality. We decided to construct them of granite blocks, like the mansion itself, and in the form of small family vaults."

"Granite outhouses?"

"Er, yes. They served their purpose quite well. But once our plumbing was fixed, we had no further need of them. We locked them up. If our pipes freeze during this storm, however, we will need them again. An inconvenience, I realize, but it can't be helped."

"Sure. It's all right. It'll be like camping."

"Exactly. Now, perhaps Miss Ursula and I can retire for the moment and allow you the opportunity to interview Paddy here. I'm not sure if you'll have time to speak with everyone tonight, but you can save some of your questions for tomorrow. Of course, I don't think there's any necessity for your questioning Dirk. He is, after all, my bodyguard."

"I guess that's OK. But I would like to talk to the guy at some point. Where is he?"

"He is already in my bedroom, guarding the door and windows." He turned to the lovely Miss Ursula Camila. "Shall we leave these gentlemen alone?"

She looked longingly at Paddy, who nodded his head and smiled at her. I watched her leave the room. Her dress was a bit tighter than necessary, and she showed off a lot of active curves. In fact, she was built like a granite outhouse.

Left to ourselves, Paddy took charge.

"Help yourself to another cigar, Axe. I'll bet you don't smoke honest-to-God Havana's every day."

"No. I think my usual cigars are made somewhere in the Florida Everglades. They taste like it, anyway."

"I'm going to have some more brandy. Sure I can't tempt you to have some?"

"No thanks. I'm on duty, so to speak. I've only got a few questions for you, and don't be offended if some of them aren't too polite. I'll be asking everybody the same kinds of questions. The whole idea is to keep Mr. Flinders safe."

"Absolutely. Absolutely. Fire away, Gridley."

"How long have you been staying in the mansion?"

"Oh, I suppose it's been close to a year."

"You're writing Mr. Flinders' biography?"

"That's right. Somebody needs to. Fascinating personality. Fascinating story. I don't mind telling you, I expect to make my fortune off the book."

"That's swell. Have you written a lot of books?"

"Well, no. Not yet, anyway. This is my first. I've been waiting for inspiration, and I've found it in Dunty."

"I see. How have you made your living in the past?"

"A little of this and a little of that. Business ventures and investments. I like to think of myself as an entrepreneur."

"Where were you living before you moved in with the Flinders?"

"That's kind of personal."

"I can't help that. I warned you that some of my

questions might not be polite."

"Well, for a time I lived with my brother, Toby, in Boston."

"And before that?"

"With my aunt and uncle, in Bolivia."

"Bolivia! That's pretty exotic. It sounds like you value family quite a lot, Mr. Cotton."

"Please, call me Paddy. Yes, you can't beat family. What they say about blood being thicker than water is absolutely correct. Don't you agree?"

"Blood is certainly thicker than water. So is ketchup. I understand that Mr. Flinders is of a generous nature. Apparently he's set up trusts for all his servants, leaving money to them when he dies."

"Doesn't surprise me. Dunty has a heart of gold. Unfortunately, hearts of gold don't always work the way they should. Dunty has a heart condition. Let's hope the world isn't deprived of him anytime soon."

"How old is he, eighty?"

"Something like that. But he's still a dynamic personality."

"Of course he is. Tell me, is there any chance that you'll inherit anything when Mr. Flinders dies?"

Paddy leapt out of his chair. "Sir, I take that as an insult! I know what you're suggesting. If you think I've invented this whole murder threat business in order to scare Dunty into having a fatal heart attack, then you're wrong."

"Maybe so. I don't believe I've got any more questions for you. On your way out would you send in your curvy assistant?"

"No, sir, I won't. I wouldn't consider exposing Ursula to your churlish questions."

"Churlish? I haven't heard that one for a while. I think your secretary can take care of herself. Send her in."

"You, sir, are lucky that the days of dueling are over."

"Sure, especially since I left my matched brace of pistols in the car. I'm always forgetting something."

Paddy stormed out. I was pretty sure he wasn't going to send Miss Camila to chat with me.

There was a big fire burning in the fireplace in the library, but there was also a big draft, even though the door was closed. I went out into the hall to see if I could find anyone who was willing to talk to poor old lonesome Axe. I didn't see anyone. I started exploring halls and passageways. The dump was big enough to hide twenty would-be murderers. Finally, I ran across Bosco. I was actually happy to see him.

"I thought you were helping the butler shovel out the latrines."

"No. They just needed airing. I hope I don't have to use one of them. Who wants to go to the can in a tomb? It's enough to make you constipated. I'm in for the night. You need something?"

"You mind my asking you a question or two?"

"Like the cops, huh? Sure, I got the time."

We returned to the library, although Bosco had to help me find it. We settled into a couple of wing chairs, the better to keep the draft off of us, and I put my questions to him.

"Don't you get tired of wearing that outfit?"

Bosco rolled his eyes and gave me a look of comic sadness. "Are you kidding? I hate wearing this outfit. I never did like it. But Cleo, the old lady, won't let me wear anything else. You ever wear tights?"

"Not since I quit the high wire act. Why don't you tell the Flinders you'd rather wear street clothes?"

"You were in the circus?"

"That was a joke. I'm not surprised you didn't recognize it."

"Oh. See, I was in the circus once. Hated it. Why don't I wear different clothes? Like I said, the old lady won't let me. But, hey, it's a living. I've got it pretty soft really. But I'm ready to try something else."

"Like what?"

"My dream is to open my own bar. I'd hire some crooner who could also play the piano, and we'd pack them in at nights. I see myself as a kind of Jerry Lewis. Me and the crooner could be the next Martin and Lewis. You know?"

"Good luck with that."

"Hey, you want to hear a joke?"

"No. Let me ask you something. If old man

Flinders kicks off, where does that leave you?"

"Right here, buddy. Cleo loves me, even if she does dress me like a sissy. Old Dunty, he don't think I'm funny. Can you believe it?"

"It's hard to. I hear that when Dunty dies the servants here will be pretty well fixed, and the ones who have been here the longest will be the best off. How long you been working for the Flinders?"

"Eight long years. Sometimes I get damned tired of it. Makes me want to tell some really off-color joke to see if Cleo will fire me. It's up to her."

"So, if Dunty dies, do you think you'll inherit enough money to open that bar you want?"

"Maybe. Nobody knows how much the old guy's really leaving us. He could make us all rich if he wanted to. He's loaded, at least for now."

"What's that supposed to mean?"

Bosco leaned forward in his chair and lowered his squeaky voice. "The old guy's losing his marbles. Some days he doesn't even remember our names. And I've heard he's making some pretty odd business deals. He was always a wiz at business, so I've heard, but you should hear some of the losing propositions he's buying into now."

"I've heard a couple of them. Are you saying he might start losing the family fortune?"

"Why not? It could happen."

"So, the sooner he turns up his toes the better your chances of getting a decent inheritance."

"That's how I see it."

"And he's got a bad ticker."

"That's the word. Though he seems strong as a horse to me."

"Do you think there's any chance one of your fellow servants is cooking up this gray toupee stuff just to try to scare the old man to death?"

"Which gray toupee? If you mean the one that was sent to Waldrous, no. That was for real. But this second toupee? It's a joke. Have you seen it? I think this whole murder-threat against Dunty is phony. One of us servants is likely behind it. But it ain't me."

"Anyone in particular?"

He lowered his voice again. "Simone. The damned bitch."

"Who's Simone, the housekeeper?"

"That's right."

"Why would she in particular want her employer dead?"

"She hates him. You should hear what she says about him behind his back. He keeps calling her by the wrong name. Tricia. That was the last housekeeper. The dead one."

"How'd she die?"

"Food poisoning. That was Abigail's fault. She poisoned all of us. She didn't mean to, it was just one of those unfortunate ragouts."

"I've eaten some of those. So, this Tricia died from it?"

"Sure, and she was Mayhew's wife. Abigail's husband, Josh, died too. Abigail was pretty upset about it. She turned in her notice, but Dunty and Cleo wouldn't hear of it. They said it was just an accident, the kind of thing that could happen to anyone. And Cleo, well, she just loves Abigail's cheese soufflés. I tell you, for a couple of weeks after the food poisoning I'd hardly eat a thing. But then I forgot all about it. That's how people are, you know?"

"Simone can't want Dunty dead just because he calls her by the wrong name. Is there anything else?"

"No. But I'm telling you, she hates the old man."

"OK. Is there anyone in the house who would especially benefit from Dunty's death?"

"That would be Cotton."

"The poor relative."

"That's right. Listen, the ladies love this guy, including Cleo. But he's getting old all of a sudden. He's losing his hair. He's getting crow's feet and bags under his eyes. He's got liver spots on the backs of his hands. I'm telling you, the guy has aged ten years in just the last few months. I think he's made some bad investments and owes money he can't pay back. And when his looks are gone, what's he got left? Ursula will leave him. Cleo will get bored with him.

"He wants to invest money in some of Dunty's crazy business deals, so he's trying to con Cleo into loaning him money. The guy's a loser. He doesn't have any money except for whatever Cleo gives him as an allowance. If Dunty croaks, I'm sure Cotton will get some money. Cleo will see to it. But it's got to happen soon."

"I'm not convinced."

"You should be a fly on the wall some days."

"I aspire to something higher."

"No, really. The way some of these people talk about old man Flinders and old lady Flinders, you'd be amazed."

"What about you? Do you ever think about helping Dunty into his grave?"

"Me? Listen, I'm a court jester, not a fool. If I tried knocking somebody off I'd get caught. I know I would. I'd end up stretching a rope. Besides, I just ain't the type. And I like the old guy. He's decent, even if he doesn't laugh at my jokes."

I stood up. Bosco stood up. We shook hands.

"Thanks for your time," I said.

"Any time. I get lonely. All I ever see are the same faces every day. Including Simone's. Yuck."

4

I walked Bosco to the door and looked around in the hall for someone else to heckle. The hall was empty. Candles burned on little tables that'd been placed here and there. I headed for the great room, thinking there would likely be people there. I was right.

Dunty and Cleo were sitting comfortably on a large love seat in front of a roaring fire. Cleo was sewing something, and damned if it didn't look like another jester's costume for Bosco. Wouldn't he be pleased. Dunty was surrounded by a heap of newspapers and was smoking a big calabash, like Basil Rathbone in a Sherlock Holmes movie. Mayhew was in attendance. He had just put down a round silver tray loaded up with crystal decanters and a pair of etched tumblers.

"I hope I'm not interrupting," I said.

"Not at all," said Dunty. "I was just enjoying a pipe by the fire. Sometimes I regret the invention of central heating. It's not as cozy as a fire somehow. What can we do for you?"

"Well, I've been rounding up folks to talk to. So far I've interviewed Paddy and Bosco, and of course Cam, but I need another victim."

"Yes, of course. Mayhew can help you with that."

Mayhew bowed my way. "A pleasure to serve you, sir."

"How about I talk to you? I know you've been busy this evening, but could you spare a few moments?"

"I am at your service, sir. If Sir and Madame will excuse me."

"We'll tend to the drinks ourselves," said Cleo. "Run along and talk to the nice detective." There was no sarcasm or condescension in her voice.

"Very well. Thank you." He bowed to his employers then turned his attention to me.

"Should we go to the library?" I asked.

"Excuse me, sir, but I found it a bit draughty earlier. I've just come in from the cold. I was out making sure Cam plowed the walks properly. Would you mind, sir, if we talked someplace else? My old bones can't abide a draft."

"Any room will do."

"I suggest the trophy room. I like to spend a bit of time there now and then. It reminds me of Mr. Waldrous, though it saddens me, too."

"Lead the way."

The trophy room was on the ground floor, like every other room I'd been in so far. Mayhew unlocked it with a key that shared space on a large ring with maybe fifteen other keys.

"I laid the fire here earlier," he said, "hoping I'd have an opportunity to pass a few quiet minutes here. Are the chairs comfortable enough for you, sir?"

"They look fine." They were all made of rattan, with cloth cushions featuring a jungle motif. I selected one not too close to the blazing fire. Mayhew, after excusing himself for sitting down in my presence, chose a chair right next to the fireplace.

"Let's begin," I said.

"With pleasure, sir."

"You've been in the Flinders' household for some time. About thirty years. Is that right?"

"Yes, sir. It is my home."

"You were here when Waldrous first received threatening letters, and then the gray toupee."

"Yes, sir. I was with him until the very last. I spent a good deal of time with him during that period."

I looked around the room. The walls bristled with primitive weapons of all kinds, chiefly knives. There were also bows and arrows, spears, and quite a few tomahawks and axes. I hoped this wasn't going to be my bedroom.

"You appear to have the confidence of your employers. Were you allowed to read any of the threatening letters that were sent to Waldrous?"

"Yes, sir. All of them."

"And you've seen the newest letter, the one addressed to Mr. Dunston Flinders?"

"Yes, sir."

"Same handwriting?"

"No handwriting, sir. The letters, both those addressed to Mr. Waldrous and to Mr. Dunty, were put together by pasting letters cut from magazines to form the words. You've heard of such missives, sir?"

"Yes. I've even seen a few. What about the postmarks?"

"There is a difference there, sir, but one easily explained. The letters to Mr. Waldrous bore postmarks from all over the world. It was clear the killer was traveling while he wrote and mailed them. He was moving closer and closer to Quartz Quarry. The most recent letter, addressed to Mr. Dunty, bears a Quartz Quarry postmark."

"Yes? So you're suggesting that Waldrous's killer has remained in the area with the idea of killing Dunty Flinders?"

"I'm sure that's the case, sir. The authorities have retained all the letters or I'd show them to you."

"It doesn't strike you that someone is simply imitating Waldrous' killer's methods to lead the police astray? To cover their own tracks when they attempt to kill Dunty Flinders?"

"No, sir. Pardon me, why would I think such a thing?"

"Well, the toupee. When Waldrous received a toupee in the mail it clearly meant something to him, though we don't know what. It shook him to his roots."

"Yes, sir, it did. He fell apart, if I'm excused for saying such a thing. I tried to help him gain back his composure. More than once I said to him: 'Buck up, sir. Buck up.' I would not ordinarily speak in such a harsh manner to one of my superiors, but trying times often require extreme measures."

"Yes. Well, I guess he didn't buck up. From what I understand, Waldrous was terrified. But Mr. Dunty has no such associations with toupees, gray or otherwise. If it hadn't been for the circumstances of his brother's death, the toupee would have meant nothing to him at all."

"I think I see what you're saying, sir, but is it an important distinction? Gray toupees may have meant nothing to Mr. Dunty before his brother's murder, but they certainly do now."

"I think you're missing the point. Waldrous' murder was likely an act of revenge. That's how I see it. Somebody hated him for what they thought was good cause. But why would that same killer hate Mr. Dunty? Just because he's related to the dead man?"

"Excuse me for pointing it out, sir, but I think you're splitting hairs."

I would have liked splitting some of Mayhew's hairs at that moment, if he'd had any, but the guy was so damned polite I couldn't get mad at him.

"OK, forget all about the rugs, the toupees. Is

there anyone in the house, servants or guests, who hate your boss or would be well-fixed if the old man croaked?"

"I'm sure I don't know, sir. And if I did know, I would not feel at liberty to reveal such things. That is not my place as a good and trusted servant."

"You're saying that if you've heard any gossip, or know anything suspicious about anyone in this house, you won't pass it on to me."

"Or to anyone, sir."

Now the guy was making me mad in spite of his impeccable manners.

"All right, then, let's talk about you. Do you like Dunty Flinders? Does he ever get on your nerves? Does he ever treat you badly?"

"Heaven forbid, sir. Mr. Dunty is as fine a master as a servant could have. I haven't a word to say against him. Or against Madam, either."

"Let's try this. If Dunty died tomorrow, would you gain by it?"

"Would I receive money, sir?"

"Yes."

"I believe so."

"And what would you spend it on. The ponies?"

"Beg your pardon, sir?"

"Horse races. Never mind. What would you spend it on?"

"Crepe and other trappings of mourning."

"What, all of it?"

"I don't know how much Mr. Dunty intends for me to have after his — shall we say — demise."

"You're a hard man to talk to, Mayhew."

"I'm sorry, sir. We all have our faults. Not, of course, that I'm suggesting you have any."

"I've got plenty, including a lousy temper. Can you round up another sucker to interview?"

"I can round someone up, yes, sir. Perhaps Abigail, the cook. She may be preparing pastry for the morning, but I'll ask her if she can spare a few minutes. Will that be satisfactory, sir?"

"Sure."

I sat and waited almost ten minutes. I thought of lighting up a cigar, but after smoking a Cuban I figured my regular brand would taste like a rolled-up road map. Mayhew finally returned, and he brought me a surprise.

"Abigail is elbow-deep in flour, sir. I've brought you Miss Ursula instead. Is that satisfactory?"

"She'll do," I said, though I was secretly delighted. The divine Ursula was standing directly behind Mayhew, like she was hiding from me. A timid girl, for all her looks. Or maybe I'm more fearsome than I realize.

"Come in and have a chair."

Ursula did just that. Mayhew bowed to us and disappeared, closing the door behind him.

"What an awful room," said Ursula, shivering. "All these sharp blades and pointy spears and things. Gosh, I'm glad there's a strong man in here with me."

OK, she was going to play the dumb girl, and I was going to be her big strong hero. That ought to puff me up like a balloon . Except I wasn't buying it.

"I have a few questions for you."

Ursula crossed her legs. Slowly, allowing one stocking top to show. Nice stockings. What was in them was pretty nice too. I noticed she was still carting around her steno pad.

"Is that for this interview?" I asked.

"Yes. I thought I'd take notes, if that's all right."

"Sure. Going to make a little report to Cotton later? Let him know just how badly I treated you?"

"You won't really treat me badly, will you?" She widened her eyes and gave me a good pout, but I wasn't interested. I felt tired and bad tempered. I wasn't going to cut this dame any slack.

"First question. Who do you know around here who would like to see Mr. Flinders dead?"

"What? Oh, my! No one would want that. He's a teddy bear. I think it's horrid someone wants to murder him. We've already had one murder here, you know. Six months ago, though it seems like yesterday."

"Next question. Who do you know around here who would come into a pile of cash when Mr. Flinders dies?"

"Why, no one. Are you talking about an inheritance?"

"Yes."

"But if Mr. Flinders dies, and I hope he won't get his poor head cut off like his brother did, Mrs. Cleo will still be alive. Everything will belong to her. Why would she give out money?" She opened her blue eyes very wide and made a little 'O' with her ruby-red mouth.

"I hear that Mr. Flinders has set up special trusts. When he dies his employees, and maybe some of his relatives, will get money. If that's true, it won't matter that Cleo's still alive."

"Oh? That sounds awfully generous of him. I know he won't be leaving me anything. Why should he? I don't work for him, and I'm not part of his family."

"Well, I guess that leaves you out in the cold." I went ahead and lit up a cigar. I knew she'd hate it. She wouldn't want her lovely perfume obscured by my cheap tobacco smoke.

"You'll be OK though," I told her. "Cotton will take care of you. You're a little more than just his secretary, aren't you?"

"Are you suggesting something improper?"

"Hell's bells! Of course not. I'm only saying that you and Cotton occasionally share the same bed. Paddy will be coming into some money. I know he's wanting it. He'd like to make some investments in wool, and buffalo, and maple syrup. He wants that money now. Think he'd bump off the old man to get it?"

Ursula stood up, a picture of steamy, seductive,

outrage. "You are a truly horrible man. I hope Mr. Cotton teaches you some manners." She turned on her high heels and swayed her hips out the door.

She'd given me exactly nothing, and that's what I'd gotten from the others. I'd been as nasty and rude as I knew how, but nobody had taken the bait and lost their temper. Somebody around this place had it in for Dunty, and I intended to find out who. I went out into the hall. Mayhew was standing there.

"I'll need to lock up the trophy room, sir," he explained.

"So soon? It's only nine. Find me one more piece of meat to grill. Is Abigail through making mud pies?"

"No need to be offensive, sir. I believe you upset Miss Ursula."

"She'll live. Come on. Who's next?"

"The household retires early, sir. Mr. Dunty and Mrs. Cleo go to bed at nine."

"Sure, they're old. But I'm sure some of the servants stay up later than nine. What about Mary Elizabeth? She's a young thing. Surely she's still wide awake."

Mayhew gave me a very dignified sigh. "I'll see who I can find, sir."

He turned his back on me and cruised down the hall, reeking of disapproval. To hell with him. I went back into the trophy room. The fire had died down some and I had quit sweating. While I waited for whoever might show up, I examined some of the weapons decorating the walls. I was busy admiring a brace of slithery-bladed Kris knives when I heard Mayhew cough discreetly behind me.

5

"I have brought you the housekeeper, Simone, sir."

"Thanks," I said, turning around. Simone certainly wasn't hiding behind the butler. She was in front of him, facing me squarely, her arms crossed over her big bosom. Her glare was steely-eyed. I was damned glad I didn't work for her. I invited her in and she sat down on the very edge of the most uncomfortable-looking chair in the room.

"You wanted to talk to me, sir?" Her voice was a treat. Like rusty nails scraped across a cheese grater.

"Yes. I just have a few questions.'

"The police already asked us questions."

"I'm aware of that, but it doesn't matter. I need to talk to everybody in this household."

Simone leaned forward in her chair and uncrossed her arms. I thought she was going to punch me. "It's an inside job, as they say on TV."

"What's an inside job, someone's wanting to

murder Mr. Flinders?"

"What else would I be talking about? You know who's behind it?"

"I'd like to know. Who would benefit most?"

"Mary Elizabeth, the little princess."

She pronounced the word "princess" as if it were the name of an especially noxious rat poison.

"How do you figure?"

"We hate her, all of us. She's Mrs. Cleo's little pet. She's become a lady's maid. She hardly does any work at all around the house. That puts a burden on me and Mavis, I'm telling you. The little princess thinks she's such a treasure, and that she's better than the rest of us. Her with her dolls' face, and her rosy skin, and her trim figure. And that hair of hers, all shining."

"I get the picture. You don't like her. But that doesn't mean she's planning to kill Mr. Flinders. What would she get out of that?"

"What wouldn't she get? Mrs. Cleo wants to adopt Marry Elizabeth. For real. She'd be set up for life. Only Mr. Dunty doesn't like it. They've got a son, a lazy so-and-so living on the continent."

"Which continent? You mean Europe?"

"That's the place. You couldn't make me live there. All those falling down buildings, and people jabbering God-knows-what languages. Brimson is his name. Stupid name. Mr. Dunty wants Brimson to inherit the entire estate. He doesn't want him to have to share with some uppity farm girl who thinks she's something. She's gone from slopping hogs and wrestling with her brothers to holding Cleo's hand."

"Sounds like this Mary Elizabeth is going to be fixed. But would she really murder Dunty to get set up as Cleo's daughter?"

"Hadn't you heard? I thought you were some kind of detective. A shyster, more than likely."

"Shyster, is it?"

"You know yourself better than I do."

"I think you're right about that. What is it that I should know that I don't?"

"Mr. Dunty's getting dotty. He's losing his memory, maybe his mind."

"He seems pretty sharp to me."

"You didn't know him before. Besides, he has his good days. He's all the time calling me Tricia. She's been dead for five years. Some days he can't remember anyone's name. Some days he thinks his brother's still alive. And he's throwing his money away hand-over-fist in stupid investments."

"How do you know that?"

"I'm not at liberty to say." She crossed her arms over her bosom again.

"Have it your way."

She leaned toward me again. "Mr. Cotton. He's the one I heard it from. When the servants are around he acts like he don't even see us. Some people treat us like that."

"Yeah, it's a big unhappy world. Wait a minute.

I got the distinct impression Cotton likes the idea of some of Dunty's investments."

"Sure, some of them. Others he thinks stink. That's why he's trying to borrow money from Mrs. Cleo She has her own fortune that nobody but her can touch. To invest. I don't know if she's going to loan him anything though. She's not under his spell like she was. He's losing his looks. And that's how he's always gotten by."

"So maybe Cotton's the one who's wanting to murder Dunty."

"He don't have the guts."

"But Mary Elizabeth does?"

"There's nothing that little trick wouldn't do. Trust me."

"I've heard Dunty has a bum ticker. Do you think Mary Elizabeth, or whoever, is hoping to scare him to death?"

"Wouldn't that be swell. You couldn't even call it murder. The little princess would love that."

"Simone, I appreciate your cooperation. You've given me a few things to think about. I think I'm through with you."

"I hope so, sir. I most definitely hope so."

She left. I went out into the hall again. Mayhew was there.

"Ready to retire, sir?" he asked.

"Yeah. Only I guess I won't be sleeping. I'm the night watchman."

"Allow me to show you to your room, sir." He took his big ring of keys and locked up the trophy room. Then he led me down the hall, across the great room, down another hall, and stopped in front of a door and opened it for me. There was a little fireplace with a fire burning in it. There were candles burning and flickering in nice silver stands. There was a double bed high off the floor. There was a closet full of clothes.

"I took the liberty, sir, of moving some of Mr. Waldrous' old clothes into your room. You're about the same size as he. The water is still running. I'll show you the lavatory down the hall. We've brought out the old pitchers and ewers from the attic, in case the pipes freeze tonight. I hope you'll be comfortable.

"Mr. Dunty's bedroom is directly across the hall from yours. My instructions were to tell you that you should keep a chair in your open doorway and keep a watchful eye out. If you hear a noise in some other part of the manor, you are to investigate it."

"OK. Tell me something. Aren't the bedrooms in old places like this usually on the second floor?"

"Yes, sir. There are still bedrooms upstairs, for guests. The servants have quarters on the third floor. Mr. Dunty and Mrs. Cleo used to have their bed chambers on the second floor, but time slows us all, and — rather than go to the expense of installing a lift — the Flinders decided to move their bedrooms to the first floor, thus avoiding having to climb stairs. The bedrooms on the second floor are now rarely used."

"Thanks for everything. Listen, I'm going to have a long night of it. I've been up since seven this morning. Any chance I could get a pot of coffee? I'll keep it on the fireplace hearth so it'll stay warm."

"Certainly, sir. Forgive me for not having thought of that myself. Abigail is still awake. I'll have her prepare some coffee for you. Do you take it with cream and sugar?"

"Black."

"Very well, sir. Allow me to show you the lavatory before I go."

He led me down the hall a few yards and opened a door that revealed a long narrow room complete with a stately toilet, a massive claw-foot tub, a pedestal sink, and a wall mirror. There were candles burning in the room.

I returned to my own quarters, dragged a wooden chair out into the hall, and sat waiting for my coffee to show up. Abigail brought it to me in a silver pot on a silver tray, complete with a china cup and saucer, linen napkin, and a knitted cozy to keep the pot warm. I thanked her. She was a plump woman in her sixties, almost more deferential than Mayhew.

Along about midnight I began to nod off. I couldn't help it. I'd been up too long, and the flickering of the candles in my room and in the hall had a mesmerizing effect on me. The damned drafts from all the different fireplaces burning in the house at the same time were making me shiver. I just wanted to climb into bed and go to sleep. That wouldn't do. I'd finished off the coffee and still wanted more. I wondered if I could find the kitchen somehow and make another pot. I needed to do something to keep myself awake.

By the light of the hall candles I could see the brass fittings of an old-fashioned telephone on a little table maybe thirty feet from me. What the hell, I'd call Tracy. She wouldn't chew my head off too badly for waking her. But when I picked up the receiver the line was dead.

Damn it, the phone lines were down.

I went into the cavernous bathroom and tried turning the water on in the sink. A little bit ran out and then stopped. The pipes had finally frozen. Great. All the coffee I'd drank was having its usual effect on me. I'd need a bathroom soon. But with the pipes frozen I'd have to go out into the storm and try to track down the private crypts and hope nobody had locked them up. I wasn't going to use the damned chamber pot one of the maids had left near my bed.

I went into my bedroom and looked around, hoping to find a flashlight. No such luck. Maybe I could find one in some other part of the house. I made my way down the hall and into the great room, guided by the candles that were still burning here and there.

I went to the front entry hall and pulled on my coat and hat. There was a drawer at the base of the coat rack, and damned if there wasn't a two-celled flashlight in it. Making my way to the back of the house, I finally found a door that looked like it might lead outside. It was locked, but with a bolt on the inside. I unlocked it and headed out into snow country.

The wind had died down some, and my flashlight showed me that the snow wasn't falling as hard as it had been earlier. After wandering around for a while I found where a path had been scooped in the snow a bit earlier. I followed it. Damned if it didn't lead to a couple of stone monstrosities that must be the outhouses. I flashed my light on one of the iron doors. Gothic letters said: "Ladies." I went to the other tomb. The door said: "Gentlemen." Close enough. I tried the door and it was unlocked. It creaked open and I found myself in an outhouse straight out of some lousy monster movie. I used it.

When I got back out and headed for the house, a tree limb broke off above me and crashed down in the snow no more than ten feet from my head. I headed back to the door I'd used to get out of the house. It was locked. I couldn't believe it. I pounded on the door for about five minutes. No body answered. Of course not. The household was asleep. The wind was blowing, rattling the windows, howling down the chimneys. Tree branches were crashing to earth. No wonder no one could hear me.

I needed to get inside soon: I'd freeze to death if I didn't. I followed the stone wall, looking for windows. I found plenty. They were casement windows and they were locked. I dug out my jackknife, slid the blade between the two halves of a window and felt around for the latch. I was lucky, I found the latch and jimmied it open with my knife. Pulling one half of the window open I dragged myself over the sill. I heard a slight whooshing sound, like a buzzard flying by my ear, and something cracked my skull hard. Some lights went on in my head and then went out.

When I woke up I realized almost at once where I was: in the room where I'd been sapped. I also knew that I couldn't have been out for long. I was draped across the window sill, half in and half out, with the window hanging open. There was snow on the floor but not a lot, and almost none of it had melted. I dragged myself to my feet and just about fell down again. I was dizzy. I explored my head with a shaking hand. There was a lump rising up on it, near my right ear, but there was no blood.

I felt around on the floor for my flashlight and found it. I hadn't switched it off, but somebody had. I clicked it on and used its beam to find the window and close it. Then I gave the room a quick search. It was some kind of conservatory with plants all over on low tables.

On the floor near where I'd been ambushed I found a wicked-looking stone axe. Maybe Indian, maybe something else. I gave it a good looking over. To hell with fingerprints, the whole Quartz

Quarry police department was likely toasting its collective toes in front of the home fire. The head of the axe must have weighed a good two pounds. There was no way someone could have hit me with it with any force at all without cracking my skull like a three-minute egg.

I stumbled around a little, still holding the axe, and found my way out into a hallway. There was a light flickering in the distance, and it was headed my way. I fumbled under my overcoat and found my Chiefs thirty-eight, then ducked back into the conservatory.

In a couple of minutes the flickering light grew level with the doorway. I shined my flashlight at it, raised my gun, and found myself facing Mayhew, dressed in a long nightgown and nightcap. He flinched at the sight of my revolver, and blinked at the beam of my flashlight, but then hurried forward with his candle.

"Sir! Sir! Has something happened?

"I'll say. I got locked out of the house when I was returning from the privy. When I crawled through a window, I got clubbed on the head. This was lying on the floor." I showed him the axe, and stuffed my gun back into my pants.

Mayhew's eyes got very big. "That's from the trophy room. I've seen it a hundred times. Praise God you aren't dead."

"Yeah, well, nobody hit me with this thing. Maybe a rubber sap, or a shoe heel, but not this."

"Where are you injured?"

"My head. I've got a knot growing on it, but the skin's not even broken."

"Quick, sir, let me help you to the kitchen to attend to your wound. We'll get it cleaned and bandaged."

He took my arm and tried helping me along, but I shook my arm free and walked on my own. The kitchen was a huge room, stone flagged, high ceilinged, and filled with stoves and refrigerators and sinks, rows of pots and pans, and everything you could possibly want for preparing meals. There was a big old wood stove in one corner, and it was glowing orange. Mayhew set his candle down and found a couple more to light.

"Don't you have more than one flashlight in this place?"

"No doubt we do, but we prefer candles. More traditional. Let me look at your head. Excuse my fingers, sir."

I excused his fingers until he started prodding my bump with them. Then I let out a yell. "I'll take care of it myself."

"Sorry, sir. I've never been much of a nurse."

"Skip it. Where were you headed when I way-laid you with my gun?"

"Investigating. A little earlier I had heard noises. First pounding, then what sounded like shouting. And after that a noise like a window banging"

"Probably banging against me while I was straddling the window sill."

"I didn't look into the matter immediately. Forgive me, sir, I thought I'd been dreaming. I wouldn't let myself believe the sounds had been real. I was too comfortable tucked into my bed. Reprehensible, really. I wasn't doing my job. I could have spared you that lump on your head."

"Skip it. At least you showed up; nobody else did. Somebody was giving me a warning. Or maybe they were trying to put a scare into folks. Don't tell anybody what happened. I want to keep this a secret."

"But surely the police must be called?"

"You better have good lungs. The phone lines are down. Also, the water pipes have frozen. Did you see anyone roaming the halls between your room and that conservatory?"

"No, sir. No one. Goodness, sir, what a trial. I do hope this storm will end soon. Perhaps you should retire, get some sleep."

"Not yet. My shift's not over. What time is it anyway?" I looked at my wristwatch. "One-thirty. What time is breakfast?"

"Seven."

"Can Abigail cook on that old wood stove?"

"Undoubtedly. She could turn out a fine meal in the jungle if she had to."

"Good, I'll be hungry."

"Perhaps you should eat something now, to fortify yourself, sir. Or, better yet, how about a drink? I'm sure Abigail has something in the pantry."

"A drink might fix me up. Make it a small one."

He disappeared into what must be the pantry,

and returned a moment later with a big bottle.

"Is bourbon all right, sir?"

"Bourbon's fine."

He found a tumbler and filled it about half full. I took it and drank down a good slug. Then I drank the rest of it.

"More, sir?"

"No. Thanks for taking care of me, Mayhew. And remember, don't tell anybody about my getting locked out and getting hit on the head."

"If you insist."

"I do. Good night."

We left the kitchen. I let Mayhew walk ahead of me and when I saw him head for a staircase I went back to the conservatory and retrieved my hat. I remembered my hat falling off when I was crawling over the windowsill, so it hadn't been on my head to cushion the blow when I'd been sapped. I returned to the great room and hung up my hat and coat, but I didn't return the flashlight to the drawer under the hall tree. I might be needing it.

6

When I found my way back to my room, some of the candles had guttered out and the fire in my room was just coals. There was a chill in the air. I threw on more logs and returned to my chair in the hall.

Between my pounding head, heartburn from too much rich food at dinner, and lack of sleep, I wasn't in an entirely chipper mood. I'd given Mayhew the stone axe, which he said he'd' put under his pillow. That reminded me that I'd seen him lock up the trophy room earlier. Somebody else had a key. Maybe the same somebody had keys to other rooms in the house. And maybe they'd been prowling around all night waiting for a dumb detective to give them the chance to knock him on the head. At least the case was getting a little interesting.

By the time the overcast sky began to lighten just a little through the window at the end of the hallway, the servants were up and stirring. I could hear them clattering around and talking in low voices in the kitchen and dining room. I left my post and went into the great room. Mayhew was putting more logs on the fire. He raised his eyebrows when he saw me.

"I'm fine," I told him, in a low voice. "Just a little bump on the noggin. Has the snow stopped?"

"No, but it has slowed down considerably. Cam has already been plowing snow. After breakfast he and Bosco will be constructing a sort of igloo by the kitchen door to store our perishables since the freezers are out of operation. Cam is also going to push a wall of snow up against Mr. Dunty's bedroom windows."

"Good idea. Let's all play Eskimo. Is Mr. Dunty all right?"

"Yes, sir. Hale and chipper this morning. Breakfast will be served presently. I suggest you retire directly afterwards."

"That's a swell idea. I'm asleep on my feet. What's for chow?"

"Sir?"

"What are we being served for breakfast?"

"Oh. I believe there will be omelets, and boiled quail eggs, and bacon and sausage, and kidney pie, and kippers. Coffee, tea, orange juice and tomato juice. Apple turnovers, and fresh fruit."

"You like to do things up right around here. Mind if I go into the dining room and start drooling?"

"By all means. There are napkins."

I found my way to the dining room. The food smells woke me up a bit. Abigail and the two maids were busy hauling breakfast to the table, and there was a sideboard piled with coffee and tea things, the dessert and fruit, and some big silver dinguses with lids that probably held enough food for Sherman's army.

My fellow diners were filing in. I took my seat next to Dirk as I had the night before. He glowered a good morning at me. I knew something about this guy, and it wasn't good. My neighbor, Blythe Bliss, was a cop, and she'd complained to me about this Dirk Drebber. He'd been on the police force in Quartz Quarry but had finally been dismissed for beating up vagrants and making passes at meter maids. Blythe had nothing flattering to say about him. Apparently he was now working for some local security service.

I wondered what bad luck had brought Mr. and Mrs. Flinders and him together. He was a beefy guy, running to fat, with hair as short as you can get it without being bald. He wore dark blue pants with a stripe on them, a blue shirt with epaulets, and had a service revolver stuck in his belt.

"Good morning, Dirk," I said, smiling brightly. "Sleep well, I hope? No bad dreams?"

"I don't dream, peeper. Ain't got the time. What about you? Was that you I heard snoring out in the hall?"

"Oh, no, that wouldn't have been me. Maybe it was the murderer."

"That's nothing to joke about, pal."

I was going to growl a reply, but all the guests had arrived and breakfast was served. Dunty and Cleo were looking their usual selves, if a bit sleepy. Cotton and his Ursula looked slick and pretty. Bosco didn't join us. I guessed he'd have to snag a bite to eat after he and Cam finished their igloo.

I ate my fill starting with coffee and muffins and working through the rest of the menu — except for the kidney pie. Who could think of eating such a thing? Dunty and Paddy talked about the old man's adolescence while Ursula took notes between bites of food. Cleo turned her attention to me and Dirk.

"Thank goodness we made it through the night," she told us, brightly. "The storm was quite a harrowing experience. Not to mention that awful madman roaming around in the dark."

At first I thought she meant me, but then guessed she was talking about Dunty's would-be killer.

"I didn't hear a thing," I said. "And I was up all night."

"You look quite tired from your vigilance. After breakfast you must go straight to bed. I believe Mayhew found some of poor Waldrous' pajamas that might fit you."

"Hope they're silk," said Dirk, with a sneer. He turned to Cleo "You'll have to excuse the bristles, missus. I didn't have no hot water to shave with this morning."

"Yes, of course. Mayhew will be bringing hot water around to the gentlemen's rooms this morning. I apologize for the inconvenience."

"Ain't your fault," growled Dirk. "The butler don't need to bring no hot water to the shamus here. He ain't got much of a beard. About like I had before I become a Boy Scout."

"You must have been quite the furry little tyke," I said. "Kind of like a young version of one of those swamp apes I hear they have in the boonies in Texas. You from Texas?"

"Do you gentlemen know each other?" said Cleo.

"I know Dirk by reputation only."

"Don't believe everything you hear, pal," said Dirk.

"You mean the things I've heard about you getting kicked off the police force?"

"I was set up. Somebody spread lies about me."

"Oh? So you didn't really wear your knuckles out on the mugs of drunks, or get a little too cuddly with the gals who patrol the parking meters?"

"All lies. Where'd you hear that crap?"

"Word gets around."

Cleo gave me a puzzled look. "I believe Dirk was injured in the line of duty."

"Sure. Maybe a meter maid hit him with her purse."

"That's enough out of you, peeper. You trying to cause trouble?"

"Not me. I'm just eating my breakfast."

"I do hope you gentlemen will get along," said Cleo. "You were both highly recommended to us. You seem crabby this morning, Mr. Hatchett."

"Just tired, Mrs. Flinders. It's time for me to hit the sack."

I wasn't in the mood for a fight. I'd have it out with Dirk later. Right now I just wanted a bed and some sheep to count. I caught Paddy's eye. He was shoveling food into his debonair craw. He gave me a glare that would have frosted over a heated branding iron. I glanced at the lovely Ursula. She tipped me a cute dimpled frown that I think was supposed to put me in my place. Dirk had gotten up from the table and lumbered over to Dunty. He was whispering something in the old man's ear. When he was through, Dunty threw a sidelong look at me and shook his head severely. I was the life of the party. I finished my last bit of bacon and excused myself. I headed off for bed.

Back in my room, I fed some more logs to the fire and donned a pair of Waldrous' silk pajamas. I'm not much for PJs, but in case of an emergency I didn't want to be parading out in the hall in my skivvies waving my shooting iron. I had just pulled down the covers on my cushy bed when there was a polite knock on my door. It was Mayhew.

"Pardon me, sir. I don't mean to interrupt your sleep, but there's something I must talk to you about."

"Yeah?"

Mayhew cleared his throat. It sounded like a well-bred cat's purr.

"Mr. Dunty wanted me to have a word with you. It seems, sir, that Mr. Dirk informed Mr. Dunty that he smelled liquor on your breath."

"I haven't brushed my teeth yet. That was pretty strong bourbon you gave me."

"Yes, sir. In view of the circumstances, will you allow me to inform Mr. Dunty and Mrs. Cleo of the little incident that occurred earlier this morning? I of course refer to your having been locked out of the house and then knocked on the head. It would explain the state of your breath in a satisfactory manner."

"Gee, I guess you're right. Go ahead and spill it to them. Tell them their swell detective got sapped."

"Yes, sir. I would feel better about telling them anyway, sir. I do not like keeping secrets from Mr. and Mrs. Flinders."

"I understand. I guess I wasn't looking at things from your side of the fence. I apologize."

"Not necessary, sir. May I say, between gentlemen, that I do not entirely approve of Mr. Dirk?"

"Fine with me. I don't know why the Flinders would hire such a thug."

"He furnished excellent references."

"I wonder how he managed that. Listen, Mayhew, could you rap on my door in a few hours? I don't want to sleep the day away."

"Certainly, sir."

"Thanks, Mayhew. You're an all right guy."

"I appreciate that, sir. Have a restful sleep."

He left and I blew out some candles and crawled into bed. Of course, I couldn't sleep. Not at first. I started thinking about things. I hate that. Who had slugged me in the night? And why?

Something interesting had happened at breakfast. Mavis had bumped into my chair when she'd been standing behind me, refilling my coffee cup. She'd said: "Excuse me, sir. Did I bump your head?" How'd she know about my head? I was sure the lump on my noggin didn't show.

Had Mayhew talked to the other servants, even though I'd asked him not to? It didn't seem like something he would do. But what other explanation was there? Surely Mavis hadn't thumped me with one of her sensible shoes. Did she know who had?

I would definitely need to keep my eyes open in this place. But not right now. I squeezed my eyes shut and thought of Tracy. Good, irascible, Tracy. My fiancée. I would have given anything to talk to her right then. Instead, I tried counting sheep. And damned if they all weren't different colors. There was even a variegated one. But that one did the trick. I fell asleep, my bruised head settled on a goose down pillow with a satin cover. Who says being a gumshoe is rough?

Unlike Dirk, I occasionally find time in my busy schedule to dream. Usually when I'm asleep. On this particular morning I had nightmares. One involved Ursula, dressed in a clingy negligee, chasing me through the convoluted halls of the manor, armed with a cat o' nine tails with candle flames on its ends. In another dream, Cam and Bosco were trying to kill me. The chauffeur was attempting to run me over in the big Rolls Royce while Bosco yelled stale jokes in my ears. It was terrifying. I was actually glad when Mayhew woke me by firmly rapping on my door.

"It is almost time for luncheon, sir," he informed me, when I opened up for him. "Did you sleep well, sir?"

"More or less. Thanks for waking me."

"I've brought you hot water, sir, if you'd like to shave and freshen up. I apologize for not being able to draw you a bath."

"I'm fine. I can always jump into the snow. The hot water sounds swell. Lunch time, huh? I'm actually hungry. I'll be ready in a few minutes."

"Excellent, sir. I've also brought you one of Mr. Waldrous' razors, and some shaving soap."

"Thanks."

I cleaned up in my room, using the pitcher and ewer, the mirror over the dresser, and the old-fashioned straight razor Mayhew had given me. It was like one of those razors Grandpa would have used, the kind you see in Westerns. I was lucky I didn't cut my throat.

I had a hard time deciding what to wear. The closet was stuffed with Waldrous' clothes, which were close to my size, but everything was too nice for me. The kind of clothes you'd wear to church, or to your wedding. I finally selected a pair of dark tweed pants, an Oxford shirt, silk socks, silk boxers, and my own scuffed shoes. I looked like the lord of the manor, but felt like Freddy the Freeloader at his own funeral.

Everyone had already assembled in the dining room. A big clock somewhere struck the hour in dour dulcet tones. I took my place next to Dirk and accidently stuck my elbow in his ribs. He grunted and gave me a sour look.

"Sorry, old top. Seems I'm a little clumsy. Maybe I'm drunk. You know how we gumshoes are. Can't stay away from the bottle to save our lives."

"So I ratted on you, what of it?"

"Nothing. You were just doing your job, like a good boy. What are we having for chow?"

Abigail had managed, somehow, to turn out quite a spread of food using that old wood stove. The cook at Rocko's, where Tracy worked, could have learned a lot from her. I wasn't as hungry as I thought, though, and more or less picked at the good food. Both Dunty and Cleo seemed a little friendlier toward me. Even Cotton's glare was a little less frosty for some reason, and I thought I caught a shy smile from Ursula.

Bosco was with us for this meal, and he looked like a man who'd just spent a lot of time out in the cold shoveling snow. He was blue around the gills and told only four or five jokes, all bad, during the whole meal. I finished up my lunch in short order and announced that I was ready to continue my interviews.

"You might wait until the servants have had their luncheon," Dunty observed.

"Of course. I hadn't thought of that. I guess they eat after everyone else has eaten. I'll just take a stroll outdoors for a while and then come back and grab one of the ladies for questioning."

I went out into the entry hall and donned my coat and hat. Both had been dried out, probably by Mayhew, which was a happy surprise. I went out the front door and discovered that while the snow and wind had lessened, the temperature had dropped at least ten degrees.

I walked along the freshly-plowed walkways and made a circuit of the house. It was a big place, and just one time around took me fifteen minutes. I figured I was starting to turn blue, so I went back inside and headed for the fire in the great room. Dunty, Cleo, Bosco, Paddy and Ursula were all there. I decided to find out more about Paddy, so I offered an insincere apology for having riled him the day before.

"I didn't mean to gravel you, I just had some questions that needed asking. With Mr. Flinders' permission, perhaps you and me could retire to the library and deplete that box of Cubans some."

7

Dunty gave us his blessing, and Paddy was willing, so we made our way to the drafty library. The whole house was drafty today, so I excused myself for a minute and went to my room and fetched a nice camel hair jacket from the closet full of the late Waldrous' clothes. I felt quite dapper when I entered the library, and I wasn't blind to the look of approval Ursula shot me. That damned Dirk was there too, sitting in a corner puffing away at a five dollar cigar like it was nothing more than one of the two-for-a-nickel stogies he generally smoked. Bosco must have stayed with the Flinders.

Paddy offered me a cigar from the humidor as if he'd paid for them himself, and graciously loaned me his guillotine cutter and gold lighter.

"How about a brandy?" He asked. "I'm having one, and so is Dirk."

"No, thanks. I'm feeling a little under the weather." I shot a dirty look at Dirk. "Make sure you don't drink more than one," I told him. He ignored me.

"I heard you got waylaid last night," said Paddy. Great, everybody knew the story. I wondered if Mayhew had spread the word or if the Flinders had passed on the story themselves.

"Yeah, I got quite a crack on the head."

"You're lucky you didn't get killed. I figure we ought to travel in pairs from now on. We've just been talking about it. Ursula and I will stick together, and Bosco and Dirk have teamed up. You'll have to find yourself a partner."

"Naw, I've got to do this job alone. That's the only way it works. I'll just have to be more cautious, and keep my gun handy."

I noticed, to my amazement, that Ursula was apparently writing all this down. What was wrong with the dame?

"I understand what it's like to work alone," said Paddy. "That's the way the business world is. Sometimes you can't trust anybody but yourself."

"I suppose that's so. I don't know much about business, and that's tough luck for me."

"Why so?"

"Well, my grandpa kicked off recently, and he left me a little money. More than I want to have just sitting around in the bank. I wish I knew more about investments."

"Say, I can help you with that. I'm in the middle of making what I don't mind saying are some shrewd investments."

"That so? I guess you've done your homework. Mind steering me in the direction of some of those investments?"

"I'd be happy to. Believe me, there's going to be plenty of profit to go around. If you're willing to trust me with some of your inheritance, I'm sure I can easily double or triple it."

"That'd be swell. Of course, you'd have to charge me for it."

"That's how it works, but I won't charge you anywhere near what those big investment firms charge. And I can get you in on the ground floor for a couple of pretty sweet deals."

"I guess you're putting all your money in them."

"Absolutely. I only wish I had more."

Paddy and I were standing near the fire, while Ursula had arranged her curves in a nearby chair. Dirk was a good fifteen feet away in another chair. Paddy leaned toward me and almost whispered. "Let's you and me get together someplace more private. Bring your checkbook."

"Sure, but I can't do it right now. My checkbook's in my car, and my car's out in the snow somewhere. Wait until the weather clears up some and you and I can talk business."

"You'll never regret it, believe me."

"I'm sure I won't. Listen, I've got to go hunt up another suspect to question."

"Is that how you think of us all? As suspects?" Paddy's tone had become less hale and hearty.

"Not really. But after getting clubbed in the head, I admit to being pretty cautious."

I excused myself, gave Ursula a bright smile, warned Dirk to stay away from the sideboard, and left the library. I figured the servants had had time to finish their allowance of beans and fatback, so I drifted over to the kitchen in hopes of finding an available Abigail.

When I stuck my head into the kitchen Abigail was washing up the dishes. She didn't see me come in and I overheard her cursing certain princesses for not being available to do their share of the kitchen duties.

"Could I have a few words with you, Abigail?" I asked, coming up behind her. She didn't jump even a mile.

"Lord, sir, you gave me a fright. Didn't your mother teach you not to sneak up on a body that way?"

"Sure, but I didn't pay any attention. Can I give you a hand with the washing up?"

"Thank you, no, sir. If you was to break any of this china there'd be hell to pay. And you wouldn't be the one blamed. It'd be me."

"OK. Don't say I didn't offer. You seem pretty scared of your employers' wrath. Do they run that tight a ship?"

"Goodness, no! The Flinders couldn't be kinder. But I already owe them more than I can ever repay. I don't want to stretch their patience."

"Are you telling me you owe them money?"

"No, nothing of the kind. It's a favor I owe them. I'd tell you the story, but it'd only bore a young fellow such as yourself."

"Now you've made me curious. Mind if we talk about it while you work?"

"Oh, if you insist. It's a sad tale, and I don't come off well in the telling. And I'm riddled with guilt, sir. Riddled fair."

"It's better than being riddled with bullets, I expect."

"You're an optimist, I can tell. Always looking for the silver lining, aren't you?"

"Sure, that's me. Every dark cloud has one you know. Even those really black ones that spew lightening and hail. No matter what happens, things can always get worse. It's my cheerful attitude that keeps me going. Now, tell me your story."

"Well, sir, I don't mean to impose on you, but it's such a sad story I can't keep myself from telling it. I've worked for the Flinders for more than twenty-five years now. No one's worked longer for them except Mayhew. We had an under butler back then, and that was my husband, Josh. We had a different housekeeper, Tricia, who was also Mayhew's wife.

"We were as happy a gathering of family servants as you could possibly have! And then came the ragout. It was a rabbit ragout, one I'd made a hundred times before, but something went amiss. I wouldn't be surprised if it was the tarragon. I never entirely trusted tarragon, and rarely use it. But as it was, I had run clean out of ground rosemary, and nothing tastes quite the same. I put the tarragon in, and the result was death for two people. Poor Josh and Tricia."

"They died of being spiced to death?"

"Well, they called it something else, the doctors and all. They called it botulism. But the tarragon helped it along, I'm sure. Imagine how upset I was. Josh and I had had a little spat, and I was still mad, but of course I wouldn't have poisoned him to save my own life."

"Of course not."

"And as for Tricia, we were like two sisters who never were. Mind, she could be bossy, but we all have our failings, I'm sure. The whole household come down with the sickness, and it was only providence that saved the most of us from dying."

"That's quite a tragic tale. Did the Flinders consider finding a new cook?"

"Oh, no, sir, not them. Such sweet folks. They stuck by me the whole time. I tried to give my notice, but Mr. Dunty and Mrs. Cleo would hear none of it. And I've been here the whole time since."

"You must feel very grateful toward your employers."

"Oh, I do, sir."

I was sorry Abigail wouldn't let me help her with the dishes. Since there was no running water it was quite a job. She was washing everything in old laundry tubs she must have dug out of the cellar. She had pots of water boiling on the woodstove so she could add hot water to the washtubs.

"Tell me, who around here would benefit if Mr. Flinders were to die early?"

"Lord bless us! No one, I would hope."

"I understand he's set up special trusts for the servants."

"Yes. He makes no secret of that."

"Who would want the money in a hurry?"

"I couldn't say. Perhaps the young ones. Young folks are always in a hurry."

"True, but — from what I understand — the longer-tenured employees will get the lion's share of the money."

"That would be me and Mayhew. Surely you aren't suggesting, sir, that either of us would plot to murder Mr. Dunty?" She grabbed a pot of scalding water off the stove and I thought she was going to throw it in my face. But she only poured it into the washtub.

"I'm not suggesting anything. I'm just collecting information."

"Do you think the police would suspect me and Mayhew if they knew about the trusts?"

"Maybe. It doesn't matter if you're innocent."

"Of course we're innocent. Though it may not look like it. Let me tell you a secret. At least, it's supposed to be a secret. Mayhew and I are thinking of marrying. But we're waiting until Mayhew retires. Then, if possible, I'll retire too. We're hoping to open a little bakery, just to help us out in our old age and to give us something to do. I guess if poor Mr. Dunty died we could use the money he leaves us for our business, but we wouldn't want such a thing, sir. Perish the thought."

"I believe you. Who else might be wanting money in a hurry?"

"I couldn't say. No one among the servants. Bosco would like to open a saloon, but he's willing to wait. He's happy with his position here. Or so he says. I don't know that Mavis or Mary Elizabeth are wanting money for anything."

"What about Mr. Cotton, or his secretary, Ursula?"

"Surely you don't think I'd know? That's their private business."

"True, but employees often pick things up, hear things. What's your take on Paddy and Ursula?"

"I shouldn't say. Really, I shouldn't."

"Go ahead. It's just the two of us here."

"Well, I think that Miss Ursula is no better than she should be. Secretary indeed. Have you noticed the scandalous way she dresses?"

"As a matter of fact I have noticed."

"And that Paddy. A gold digger. I know men aren't often called such things, but the name fits him."

"There aren't any eligible wealthy women around here."

"Not in the manor, no, but in town. Who knows

what he does when he's not here? And the way he fusses over Mrs. Cleo you'd think she was the real Cleopatra. And, worse, he's trying to borrow money from her. The cad!"

"He wants to invest in some of Mr. Flinders' business projects."

"Yes, and I guess that's a way to keep the money in the family, so to speak. But it's shameless the way he tries to feed off others. I'll be happy when the man moves on, though I shouldn't say it."

"How bad is Mr. Flinders' heart? Do you think it's possible someone could actually scare him to death?"

"Goodness, yes. He came close to dying when Waldrous was murdered. What a horrible time that was, sir. He had a small heart attack. We could have lost him. If you could just track down who's behind all this business of threatening folks with toupees I'm sure we'd all thank you for it."

"I'm trying, but I don't have much to go on."

"How's your head, poor man?"

"Does everybody know about that?"

"Mr. Dunty told everybody, yes. He wants us all to watch over you."

"Swell, a house full of guardian angels. Speaking of angels, where are Mavis and Mary Elizabeth right now?"

"Mavis is doing the rooms with Simone. Hard work it'll be, too. What with no electricity, or water to speak of, and doing everything by candlelight. The princess will likely be with Mrs. Cleo, being petted."

"I need to talk to both of them. When Mavis is finished with her cleaning, and you see her, could you send her to the library for me?"

"I will, sir."

"Thanks. And thanks for your time. I think I'll hunt up Mary Elizabeth."

"Good luck prying her away from Mrs. Cleo, sir."

I left the kitchen and wandered out to the great room. Dunty and Bosco were there, but no one else.

"Where's your bodyguard?" I asked Dunty.

"He is presently checking the passages between the walls of the manor. You should probably be doing that once a night as well. Have Mayhew show them to you."

"Passages in the walls? You mean like secret passages?'

Dunty gave me a hoarse laugh. "No, passages designed to allow the servants to move from one part of the house to another without disturbing anyone. The place is honeycombed with them. When my brother Waldrous started receiving death threats, one of the first things we did was have some of those passages blocked up. But we had to leave some of them open for practical reasons. The servants use them every day.

"Bosco here is guarding me until Dirk returns. He's armed with the fireplace poker. I suggest you take a nap after dinner; you'll need more sleep before your night vigil. Oh, and do be careful to-night."

"Don't worry. I'll look after myself. By the way, Mr. Flinders, where would I find Mary Elizabeth about now? I need to talk to her."

"Well, Cleo is lying down for an hour or so and Mary Elizabeth is reading to her." He cleared his throat. "Really, though, Cleo and I see no necessity for your interviewing Mary Elizabeth. We've changed our minds about that. She's a frail, sensitive, girl. Why don't you simply cross her off your list?"

"That won't work. It isn't fair, for one thing. And for another, I need to question everyone who lives or works here. That's the way I do things. You hired me for a job and I'm going to do my damnedest to perform it. I won't harm Mary Elizabeth. I doubt if I'll even make her faint."

"Well, perhaps you should talk to Cleo about the matter."

I was about to argue some more when Dirk lurched into the room carrying an entire candelabra.

"Everything safe and sound?" Dunty asked him.

"Natch, Mr. Flinders. It's all safe. Did you tell the shamus here about the rat tunnels you've got in this house?"

"Yes, and Mayhew will show them to him."

"Now that Dirk's back," said Bosco, "Mind if I take Mr. Hatchett here into the billiard room for a couple of games of pool? I've worked awfully hard today, Dunty."

I gathered that Bosco had the same immunity to bad manners that court jesters of old enjoyed. I couldn't imagine Mayhew or Abigail calling the old man "Dunty" without being reprimanded. Dunty acted like he hadn't even noticed the familiar form of address.

"By all means. Play as long as you like. Enjoy yourselves."

"You up for a game of eight ball?" Bosco asked me.

"Sure, I wouldn't mind a game, as long as we aren't betting money."

"Let's go."

8

Bosco led me to a room about three rooms past the library. It was big and airy, with its own fireplace. The fire had burned pretty low, so Bosco threw on another couple of logs. Then he went over to an ornate cabinet in one corner and rummaged around until he found a crystal decanter full of amber-colored liquid, and a couple of glasses. They must have liquor in every room in this place. Bosco poured himself a stiff one.

"Drink?" he asked.

"No thanks."

"Not much of a drinker, are you?"

"Not in this place."

"Let's play pool."

There was a rococo-looking pool table. Bosco grabbed the triangle and racked up the balls. We both selected cues from a rack on the wall and chalked them up.

"You break," said Bosco.

I broke. The seven ball went into a side pocket.

"Solids. Keep going," said Bosco.

I kept going. I called the three in the corner and missed.

"My turn."

"Say, where's Cotton and his slinky assistant?"

"In the old man's office. Ursula's typing up some of Dunty's stories and I guess Paddy's supervising. He's big on supervising. He's what I wanted to talk to you about." He tried for the fifteen ball in the side and missed. My turn.

"What's up about Paddy?"

"Well...guess what I helped old silk-drawers Paddy do this morning?"

"Watch what you say about silk drawers, I'm wearing some of Waldrous's. What'd you help Paddy do?"

"You heard the old man talking about blocking up some of those servant's passages? Well, there's one in Paddy's room. There's a little door next to his closet. He had two big trunks filled with about a ton of scrap metal in front of them. I helped him move them."

"Interesting." I sank the two ball. "What'd he want to do that for?"

"He let out the big secret. He and Ursula are an item, and he wants a way to sneak into her room at nights. He and Ursula managed to unblock the door in her room, but he didn't need my help for that."

"I wouldn't think Paddy and Ursula's playing at Noah's Ark would be much of a secret."

"It isn't. Everybody knows. So why all of a sudden can't he just walk down the hall to her room like he usually does?"

"You got me. Do you think he's cooking up some plan to scare the old man?"

"I'm thinking maybe. He cautioned me not to tell anyone about helping him unblock the door. Even offered me a bribe: stock in some company he's starting. Probably worth exactly nothing. But here's something else. I heard about you getting sapped last night."

"Talk about big secrets."

"Yeah, well, I might know who did it."

"You kidding? Who?"

"The same guy. Mr. Smooth Operator. I need another drink."

"You look done in, pal."

"I'll say. I shoveled enough snow today to make a snowman the size of the Statue of Liberty. Say, did you hear the one about the two nuns and the Statue of Liberty?"

"Save it for Cleo."

"Suit yourself."

"What makes you think Paddy knocked me on the head?"

"I couldn't sleep last night. I think it's because I saw that new outfit Cleo's sewing for me. Anyway, I was lying awake most of the night. Sometime early this morning the wind died down for about a minute. I heard a door in the hall squeak open. Mayhew should oil the hinges."

"Paddy's door?"

"Ursula's. But the footsteps that came down the hall weren't hers. Too heavy. So I figured Paddy was going to freeze his can going out to the communal tombs to take a leak. But then when I heard about you getting ambushed, I had another thought.

"What if Paddy had been checking up on you, for whatever reason? If he'd seen you sitting in your chair he could have told you he was headed for the family vaults to do some mourning. Maybe that's really why he got up. But if he saw your chair empty he might have put two-and-two together. So he finds the door you went out of, 'cause it's unlocked, and he locks it. The wind's howling again by then, so he figures nobody will hear you when you pound on the door and start howling to be let back in."

"That's pretty much what happened."

"How did you get back in?"

"I jimmied the latch on a window."

"So maybe Paddy heard you doing that. He sneaks up on you and clubs you with that stone baseball bat or whatever it was."

"It was a stone axe, and nobody hit me with it. They left it lying by me to make it look like that was the weapon. But, believe me, even a tap from that thing would have cracked my skull."

"OK. So maybe that's what he did. He sent a message to you that this place ain't a safe one for you to hang around. And he gets to scare the old man, knowing he'll find out about it."

"I like it. But there's one thing wrong."

"What's that, brother?"

"That stone axe. It was from the trophy room. I saw Mayhew lock up that room hours before I got sapped. There's no other way to get into the trophy room except the windows, and they're barred."

"For real? That does throw a monkey wrench into things, don't it?"

"Don't feel bad. You might still be right. Maybe Paddy got hold of a key somehow. Maybe he knows how to pick locks. It's not that hard. I've done it. Tell me something, what do you know about Mavis?"

"Maybe more than I'm supposed to. I slip down to her boudoir some nights."

"That a fact? Think she might have conked me on the head?"

"No. Why?"

"Because she knew about my being sapped at breakfast. I hadn't told anybody but Mayhew, and I'd asked him to keep quiet about it. She bumped into my chair and said something like: 'Sorry! How's your head?'"

"That's damned funny. This whole place is funny."

We played three games. I won two out of three. Then I remembered Mavis.

"I think Mavis might be waiting for me in the library," I told Bosco. "I better get over there."

"She won't wait for you long. That girl doesn't have a lot of patience."

We both left the billiard room and walked along to the library. The door was open. I could hear a soprano hiss cursing certain detectives for standing someone up. I looked at Bosco. He shrugged.

"Guess I'll be seeing you," he said, and moved along in the direction of the great room. The hall was drafty. There were icy currents of air swirling around everywhere. I shivered and stepped into the library.

"Where you been?" Mavis greeted me. "I've been here ten minutes, at least. I'm a working girl, you know? I got to get back to work."

She was standing in front of the fireplace. She walked toward me and I sized her up. Her shoulders were arched back and her too-wide mouth had a sneer on it. It was a cute face, but nothing special. Her walk was something though. She could have used those hot hips to recruit sailors.

"Sorry. Time kind of got away from me. I've only got a few questions for you."

"Have a drink," she offered.

"No thanks."

"Pour one for me then."

"You're on the clock."

"Tell me about it. Pour me a stiff one."

I went over to the liquor cabinet and fixed her a big brandy and water. She drank it down like a champ. She took a roll of breath mints from a pocket of her maid's outfit and popped a couple in her mouth.

"Don't get the idea that I make a habit of drinking on the job," she said. "But these are tough times."

"Sure. First question. How'd you know I'd been hit on the head? I mean, you knew at breakfast before anyone else knew."

She gave me a scared look. "What are you suggesting? I didn't know about your being conked on the skull! At least not at breakfast. I was talking about something else. I figured you had a hangover."

"From drinking too much coffee?"

"I was in your room this morning, refilling your pitcher of water to wash in. There was an empty whiskey bottle by your bed. What was I supposed to think?"

"Somebody planted that bottle. Maybe that Dirk goon. He wants to make trouble for me. I don't think he likes the competition."

She shrugged some nice shoulders. "Sure, if you say so."

"OK, never mind that. Next question. If Mr. Flinders died tomorrow, how well fixed would you be?"

"Who knows? I might get a couple of bucks. I think that whole trust malarkey is just a way to get us to work harder and not look for other jobs. That's how it looks to me. I'm not counting on nothing much from the old man. I mean, Mr. Flinders."

"Call him what you like, I won't tell. Who needs money around here?"

"We could all use some dough." She put her hand on her little apron, over her stomach, and I noticed she was carrying a couple of extra pounds around the middle.

"You married?" I asked.

"You interested?"

"I'm just asking a question."

"Nobody in this house is married except the Flinders. They don't like married servants I guess."

"Mayhew and Abigail had spouses."

"Yeah, but not anymore. I think Cam might have a wife, or at least has a woman, tucked away in the carriage house, but he keeps it from the Flinders."

"What business is it of theirs? Do they really prefer single servants?"

Another shrug. "Maybe. I don't know. They might figure we work better if we don't have husbands or wives to fuss over."

OK. Who would want to scare Dunty to death?"

"Nobody. He's a sweet old guy when he can keep his hands off a girl."

"He handles you?"

"Not so you'd notice. But, yeah, his hands get away from him sometimes. Just ask the princess."

"I will, if I ever see her. What's your take on Mary Elizabeth?"

"Just a girl who's found herself in the right spot. Cleo fawns all over her. Wants to adopt her. Who wouldn't want to be adopted into a rich family?"

"Are the rest of you jealous of her?"

"Some might be. I don't care, myself. We get along. You got any more questions?"

"A couple. What do you know about Paddy and Ursula?"

"Nothing. Ursula's OK. Paddy's got his nose up in the air. He thinks he's better than the servants, but is he? He's just a moocher if you ask me. I'll be happy when he's gone."

"And when will that be?"

"Ask him. He's got plans, but I think he's sticking around. He's making his move on Mary Elizabeth so that when she's adopted he'll be fixed. Wants to marry her I think."

"What does she think of that?"

"She thinks he moves too fast. I wouldn't be surprised if she's complained to Mrs. Cleo about him. But maybe not. The old lady would boot Paddy out in a hurry if she thought he was bothering her little princess."

"What if she found out about you and Bosco?"

That made her mad. Her nostrils flared and she practically spit words at me.

"That little louse! What's he doing, bragging? I'll fix his wagon for him. I figure what a girl does on her own time is her business. I ought to dump Bosco like a hot brick. If it wasn't for the singing

I'd — "

"Go on. What singing?"

"It's like this. Bosco wants to buy his own bar. He wants to tell jokes to an audience of drunks every night. He wants a piano player who can sing, but I don't like that idea. See, I can sing, I really can. I'm pretty good. I want him to hire a piano player, but I want to do the singing. Bosco's almost sold on the idea. I practice my singing in the library at nights. That room is practically soundproof. Bosco sneaks in and listens sometimes. He thinks I'm quite the canary."

"So if Dunty gets scared to death in the next few days, or weeks, you and Bosco can make your dreams come true."

"Don't get any dumb ideas. I don't know who's wanting to kill the old man, but it's not me, and it's not Bosco. Bosco doesn't have the guts, and I'm not the murdering kind."

"I'm not accusing either one of you of anything. Thanks for your time. I think I'm finished with you."

"About time. Watch your head when you're creeping around the house tonight."

"I'll watch out for every part of me, don't worry."

Mavis left the room. I watched her. It was fairly entertaining.

I couldn't decide if I should take a nap before dinner or after. I was tired, but dinner would be served in about an hour and a half. That wouldn't give me enough time to sleep, so I decided to wait until after the meal. In the meantime, I thought I'd look up Mayhew and have him introduce me to the servants' magic passageways. I headed out to the great room again. Dunty and Cleo were there. Dirk and Bosco were there. Mary Elizabeth was nowhere to be seen. I asked Cleo about that.

"Where's your little princess, Mrs. Flinders?"

"Helping Abigail in the kitchen. Why, Mr. Hatchett?"

"I'd like to speak with her, if I might."

"That won't be necessary, Mr. Hatchett. I can vouch for Mary Elizabeth's character. She's an innocent girl and can't possibly have anything to do with the threats made against my husband."

"I wasn't suggesting that she's involved in the murder plot, Mrs. Flinders, but she might still possess information that can help me find whoever the would-be killer is."

"Nonsense. I want you to leave the girl alone."

"I'm only trying to do my job."

"Doing your job means doing what I ask you to do and not doing what I ask you not to do."

That put me in my place, but not for long. She'd made me more determined than ever to have a chat with the princess. I turned to Dunty.

"Do you know where Mayhew is, Mr. Flinders? I'm ready to have him show me those servants' passages now."

He picked up his schoolmaster bell and jingled it. Somewhere out of the woodwork the butler appeared.

"May I be of service, sir? Madam?"

"Yes, Mayhew," said Dunty. "Please give Mr. Hatchett a tour of the inner hallways used by the staff. I want him to keep an eye on them during his night watches."

"Yes, sir." Mayhew turned to me. "This way, sir."

He led me into the cavernous pantry just off the kitchen. He opened a narrow door and handed me a lighted candle in a holder, then took one for himself.

"Lead on," I told him.

The passage was narrow and not very high. Here and there was a bare light bulb, useless now, sticking out of a wall socket. The floor was heavily carpeted, the better to allow the help to go about their spelunking quietly. There was a musty smell, and damned if there wasn't a cold draft in the passage. Our candles flickered and even threatened to go out.

Mayhew showed me several doors opening off the main passage that he said had been blocked off at the time of Waldrous's troubles. He assured me they were still blocked off. We finally came to a steep staircase that led up to the second and third floors. It also led down to the cellar.

We went up first, all the way past the third floor and up beyond into the attic. Mayhew opened a door to show me the attic's interior. It was cluttered with old furniture, trunks, boxes, you name it. Next we went down all the way to the cellar. It was like a catacombs or something. It wasn't as cluttered as the attic, but there was still plenty of stuff in it.

"The laundry facilities are down here," Mayhew told me, gesturing at two washing machines flanked by two dryers. There were also some clotheslines stretched across here and there.

"What's that?" I asked, pointing to what looked like a big bulls eye painted on an upright sheet of plywood.

"For knife throwing practice, sir. Abigail is quite accomplished at the sport. She brings the other ladies down here periodically to let them practice. Abigail is a firm believer in a lady's being able to defend herself."

"What ladies are we talking about?"

"Simone, Mavis, Mary Elizabeth. Even Miss Ursula."

"Swell. Remind me to not make any of them mad, if I haven't already done so."

"They would never harm you, sir."

"Somebody sure tried to harm me last night. Are you sure all those doors you said were blocked are still really blocked off?"

"Yes. The maids would have noticed when they were doing the rooms."

I found that interesting. Perhaps Paddy had removed the contents of the heavy trunks, chucked the stuff into the closet, and set the empty trunks back in front of the little door leading from his room to the servants' passage. I wanted to know what he was up to.

"Are you confident you can find your way around in these passages tonight, sir?"

"Yeah, I think so. I'll holler my lungs off if I get lost."

"Do be careful, sir. No one knows better than you that treachery and danger are afoot."

"Believe me, I won't let that slip my mind. Let's go back upstairs."

We returned to the pantry and the kitchen.

"Dinner time is approaching, sir. You might want to get ready."

"Get ready? You mean tie on a bib?"

Mayhew cleared his throat, a melodious sound. "I meant that you should change your clothing, sir. Dinner dress. And different—ah—shoes."

"You want me to put on a monkey suit to eat? Sure, but that's not what I'm used to."

"Well, sir, when in Rome — "

"Yeah, yeah, I got you. When in Rome do what the Romanians do. I'll get dressed."

9

I'm always a little rebellious. When I got up to my room I couldn't quite make myself put on one of Waldrous's swell dinner costumes. I left on the tweed pants and my own admittedly scuffed brown shoes. I put on the least attractive dinner jacket I could find, though it was still nicer than anything I'd ever worn before. I also found what I considered to be a pretty silly tie with fat diagonal stripes. I tied it as badly as I know how. I splashed some water on my face and hands from the replenished ewer, slicked down my hair a little, and I was ready.

It was still a few minutes before dinnertime, so I stretched out on the bed, hoping I wouldn't fall asleep. I didn't. I heard the dinner gong go off and headed for the dining room.

Mayhew was right; everybody was dressed up. I hadn't noticed that the night before. Unfortunately for Bosco, he was still wearing his silly jester's outfit, and Dirk, God bless the goon, was decked out in his usual phony cop costume, but he had his napkin tied around his neck, which kind of hid the gun stuck in his belt. He'd need the napkin, the guy had the table manners of a wild hog. Nobody looked at either of us funny, which showed what good breeding can do.

The meal was great, but I was tired of well-cooked food. I yearned for a greasy egg sandwich from Rocko's. That made me think of Tracy. When was I going to see her again? The phones were still out so I couldn't even give her a holler on the horn.

Whether it was because of the draftiness of the old manor, or the tension caused by the death threat against Dunty, everybody but me drank a whole lot of wine with their meal. Dirk chugged like a seaman on leave. Even Cleo was getting pretty tanked up. I watched, nursing my coffee, while the diners' faces turned more and more flushed and their eyes stopped focusing clearly. Maybe everyone, including the would-be killer, would sleep well tonight. That could make my job easier.

When the meal was finally over I headed off to bed while the others went off to the library or wherever. I was in luck, I ran into Mary Elizabeth as I was passing through the great room.

"Just the girl I wanted to see," I told her, cheerily. She cringed.

"Begging your pardon, sir, I'm quite busy."

"Are you? I won't take up much of your time, I

promise."

"Mrs. Cleo doesn't want me talking to you, sir. Excuse me."

I sidled over and cut off her exit.

"It will only take a couple of minutes. What Mrs. Cleo doesn't know won't hurt her. And if one of us gets in trouble it won't be you. Let's just step into the conservatory and have our little chat."

"I'm allergic to flowers, sir."

"That's OK, I don't mind your sneezes. This way, please."

I guided her by the elbow into the unoccupied conservatory where somebody had sapped me the night before. We found chairs near the fireplace and I threw some additional wood on the fire. I looked at the young maid. She was certainly something to look at. Young, pretty, liquid-eyed, shimmery-haired, with a slight but undoubtedly feminine figure. No wonder they called her the princess.

As soon as I started talking to her she lowered her gaze to her lap where she held her clasped hands. I felt like a heel, but why?

"How's life in the old Flinders' manor?" I asked.

"Wonderful, sir. That is, except for what's happened to poor Mr. Dunty. It's pretty harrowing. Don't you think?"

"Harrowing as all get out. Sure. But you're doing OK, right?"

"It's a wonderful place to work, sir.

"I imagine. Are all the servants as happy as you?"

"I don't know why they wouldn't be."

"Is there anyone who might want Mr. Dunty dead?"

"Oh, no, of course not! Only the killer, and he's not one of us."

"Maybe. I've heard a few things around here. Sounds like you might be pretty well fixed soon, if the Flinders are thinking of adopting you."

"Mrs. Cleo would like that, but I don't think Mr. Dunty wants a daughter, not really."

"So, if you, or somebody, put the old man in his grave, you and Mrs. Cleo would be running the show around here."

"That's a horrible thing to say." She raised her eyes for a second and tried to put some steel into her gaze. It didn't work. She didn't even manage aluminum foil. "I'm not afraid of you."

"Who said you were? Who'd be frightened of kindly old Uncle Axe? Has Mr. Dunty ever visited you in your room at night?"

"Of course not! How can you think such a thing?"

"What would you do if he did visit you?"

"I'm not helpless, you know. Abigail taught me how to throw knives. Her husband used to throw knifes for fun and he taught her how. And I keep a baseball bat by my bed. I played on the girls' team in high school. I could knock it out of the park."

"Sure you could. So Mr. Dunty's never laid a

hand on you?"

"No. Not even when we're alone. I give him knitting lessons in his office most days, and he behaves like a perfect old gentleman — he wants to learn because of some investment of his."

"What about Mavis? Has he ever gotten cozy with her?"

She was silent.

"Answer the question."

"Only once, recently, and that didn't mean anything. Not what you're thinking. He put his hand on her tummy, just the other day. He said: 'I hope a little one's not on the way.' It's funny in a way." She actually laughed, like Santa's sleigh bells ringing way off in the distance. "Mavis has put on a little weight. It's because of Abigail's caramel pecan pies. Mavis can't resist them."

"I'm sure they're very tasty. Anybody around here needing money right now? I don't mean just the servants."

"I should think everyone around here would be quite content just the way things are"

"What about Paddy Cotton?"

"I hardly know him."

"No? He hasn't made any passes at you?"

"A lot of men make passes at me. It doesn't mean anything. They're just being friendly. That's how men are."

"Yeah, we gents are mighty friendly. Do you have any idea who sapped me last night? I'm sure you've heard about it."

"I'm sure it was an accident. I mean, someone was scared and thought you were an intruder. And then they were too embarrassed to admit it later."

"Sure. Hitting a guy on the head with a stone axe is pretty embarrassing. How many folks in this joint have keys to all the doors?"

"I wouldn't know. Mayhew, and Simone, but I don't know who else."

"All right. I guess I'm finished with you."

"I might have to tell Mrs. Cleo about your making me talk to you like this. I don't like keeping things from her. But I wouldn't want you fired."

"Tell her whatever you want, as long as it's true. I can take care of myself."

We left the conservatory. Mary Elizabeth hurried away down the hall, and I went to my room for some much-needed sleep. When I got to my door I was surprised to see Mayhew standing in the hall.

"Excuse me, sir, I thought I'd wish you a good night. When would you like your wake-up call?"

"Nobody needs to go to the trouble to wake me up. Don't you have an old alarm clock I can borrow?"

"It is part of my duties to be available when needed, sir. Tell me when you want to be awakened. I'll have a fresh pot of coffee made for you."

"OK. Thanks. I guess nine o'clock will do."

"Certainly, sir. Oh, and I have something for you." He turned and took a bell like the one the

Flinders used to summon Mayhew and handed it to me. "If you need anything, sir, ring me. Please. Anything at all."

"That'd wake up the whole house."

"These are difficult times. It is imperative that you summon me if I'm needed. Don't forget last night, sir."

"All right, I'll take the bell, but I'll only ring it in an emergency."

"Very good, sir. Good night."

I took the bell and went into my room. I undressed, put on Waldrous's PJs, and placed my revolver on the nightstand where it'd be handy. I blew out all the candles but one and climbed into bed. I went to sleep in a hurry.

It seemed like only a minute later when Mayhew rapped at my door. I got out of bed groggily and opened for him.

"Nine o'clock, sir." He set a tray down on the little round table where candles burned right outside my door. "Coffee, sir, and some biscuits, that is, cookies."

"Be as British as you want, Mayhew, it doesn't bother me. Thanks for everything."

"You're most welcome, sir. Don't forget to ring the bell if you need me."

"I'll be fine, thanks."

He wandered away, not making a sound. I spent the first couple of hours of my watch alternately sitting in my chair and pacing up and down the halls. It was boring. The wind had come up and was howling like starving wolves outside. I wondered if it'd started snowing again.

At the stroke of midnight I decided it was time to check out the servants' hallways. I took my flashlight and my gun and headed for the kitchen. I went through the little door off the pantry and prowled around in the first floor passage. I didn't see anybody or hear anything.

I walked up the narrow stairs to the second floor, then the third, and ended up in the attic. I used the flashlight to give the attic a good looking over. There was so much junk piled and stacked everywhere that you could have hidden a platoon of soldiers there. I didn't see anyone, so I headed back downstairs.

When I reached the second-floor landing and started down the next flight of steps, I tripped on something and — to use a British expression — went arse-over-teacup down the stairs. I ended up down in the cellar. How I kept from breaking my fool neck I'll never know. I was pretty lucky. Some sore ribs, a bruised knee, and a slightly-sprained right wrist completed the list of my injuries.

I'm not that clumsy, at least I don't think I am. Something was up. I found my flashlight, still shining, near one of the washing machines. Fortunately, it had landed on a pile of dirty laundry and hadn't broken. I took it with me up to the second-floor landing.

I'd been right. A booby trap had been set. Someone, no friend of mine, had stretched a length of wire about six inches above the top step, fastened on each side with cup hooks screwed into the walls. I took my jackknife and managed to saw through the wire, cursing whoever had done this to me. Then I hobbled back to my post outside my bedroom door.

I was twitchy as hell by now. So, it's no surprise that I jumped out of my chair almost high enough to bump my head on the ceiling when I heard a strange noise from somewhere in the house. It was a scraping, rasping noise. I grabbed my flashlight and gun and went to investigate. I thought the noise might have come from the great room or the dining room. I checked both and found nothing. It hadn't been my imagination, and it hadn't been a noise from outside. It was getting to be a creepy night.

I had almost reached my chair in front of my bedroom door when I felt something whistle past my ear that wasn't a draft. I hit the floor, switched off my flashlight, then alligator-crawled a few feet to the table near my chair. I used my arm to brush the candleholder to the floor, putting out the flame.

I stayed on the floor a good five minutes. I didn't hear a thing. I risked trying the flashlight again and swept the passage both ways. Nothing. At least, no ghouls or murderers. But there was something sticking in the door at the far end of the hallway. I got up and walked that way and examined the door.

There was an arrow sticking out of it. It was time to ring Mayhew's bell, but I didn't have to. At that moment a yell, or scream, or wail, filled-up half the house like the dying cry of an overgrown goblin.

The hallway filled up in a hurry. Doors banged open and people appeared in their night clothes, some of them hastily pulling on robes and wrappers. First it was Dirk and Dunty, then Cleo. Paddy and Ursula both came out of Ursula's room. The young secretary was clad in a silk gown as full of peep holes as a giant doily. I remembered the dream of her chasing me in a negligee, armed with a cat-o-nine-tails. Dressed the way she was now, I'd let her catch me. In a couple of minutes the servants started showing up. I was the center of attention until Dunty suddenly clutched at his heart and started gasping.

"Get his nitroglycerin," screamed Cleo, "and brandy."

"And my pipe," croaked Dunty.

Mayhew took off to retrieve the requested medications.

"What happened out here?" snarled Dirk. He was supporting the old man with one beefy arm and looked very noble.

"All hell broke loose," I explained. "Somebody shot an arrow at me and then screeched like a banshee."

Mayhew returned with the pills, the pipe and tobacco, and a bottle and glass. I dragged my hall chair over for Dunty to collapse in.

Cleo filled the glass half-full of brandy, fumbled a pill into Dunty's craw, and made him swallow. Mayhew was busy stuffing tobacco into the calabash. He turned to me.

"Are you all right, sir?" he asked, solicitously.

"Sure, I've just got a banged-up knee, some sore ribs, and a sprained wrist. I'm swell."

"Whatever happened, sir?"

"Somebody booby trapped the servants' stairs and I took a tumble."

Dirk guffawed, showing some nice gold teeth way back in his mouth.

"Drunk again, are you? Let me smell your breath." He stepped close and I stepped back.

"Get away from me, you bum. You aren't sniffing my breath. I'd sooner be kissed by a hyena."

"Allow me, sir, if you don't mind."

"Sniff away, Mayhew."

He came up close and took a discreet snuffle. "Curried lamb," he announced.

"Pretty strong stuff that curried lamb," sneered Dirk. "It'll cover a lot of sins."

"Maybe you should rub it all over your body," I said.

He came at me and poked at my jaw. I leaned away from the punch and gave him a hard right. I'd forgotten my sprained wrist, but I remembered it now. I howled.

Dirk laughed. "Pretty hard jaw, huh?"

I came at him again, threw a left hook at his

face, followed it with a left uppercut to the chin. It rocked him on his heels and he lost his smile. Mayhew and Paddy stepped between us.

"Gentlemen, please," said Mayhew, "some decorum."

"Break it up you two," said Paddy.

I glanced at Ursula. She was panting. Simone screamed, for no particular reason. It sounded like a train coming to a quick stop. Dunty had recovered some and was saying breathlessly: "Not in my house, sirs. Not in my house."

I got ahold of myself. "Then keep your pet ape off me."

"Your injuries need attending to," said Mayhew. He turned to Dunty. "Are you all right, sir?"

Dunty was puffing at his pipe now. He looked contented if a bit pale.

"I'll be right as rain in a moment. Please take Mr. Hatchett to the kitchen and take care of his wounds."

"Let's take a look at this arrow first," I said. I waded through the crowd and unstuck the arrow from the door. It wasn't an Indian arrow. It was fletched with toucan feathers, or something equally exotic. The shaft was made from some kind of reed. The arrowhead was beautifully-knapped stone. It would have looked lovely sticking out of the back of my neck.

There was a scroll of paper tied around the shaft. I removed it and unrolled it. There were words on it, made of letters cut from a magazine.

The message, which I read out loud, said: "First your detective dies, then you, Mr. Dunstan Flinders. You cannot escape the wrath of the gray toupee."

That got a reaction. Dunty pawed at his heart again. Simone treated us to another scream. Mayhew murmured "Lord have mercy." Mary Elizabeth squeaked: "It's not fair! Poor Mr. Dunty."

"I think it would be best if everyone returned to their rooms," said Cleo, in a queenly voice. "We'll discuss this over breakfast."

10

Folks reluctantly dispersed, mumbling and casting backward glances as they moved along towards their separate bedrooms. Bosco, dressed in some kind of court jester pajamas, appeared at my elbow.

"Let me help you patch up Axe," he told Mayhew.

"Come along then, sirs." He led us along to the kitchen. He ducked into the pantry and came back with gauze, iodine, adhesive tape and bourbon. I looked longingly at the whiskey bottle.

"None of that for me, thanks. I've already got a reputation as a drunk around here."

"It will quiet your nerves and dull the pain," Mayhew insisted. "Mr. Bosco and I will vouch for your having taken the bourbon against your will."

"Sure," said Bosco. "And I won't mind taking a snort myself. I'm a little shaky. Was that arrow really intended for you, Axe?"

"It whistled past my ear, but there's no way of

knowing how expert the archer was. Those bows and arrows are tough to shoot. I know, I've tried."

"Let's start with your knee," said Mayhew.

I rolled up my pants leg, noticing a big hole ripped in Waldrous's nice tweed trousers. The knee cap was scraped and swollen. Mayhew applied iodine and it stung like hell. Next he felt of my ribs and I wanted to kill him. I took off my shirt and he wound about thirty yards of adhesive tape around my chest. That was going to feel great when I pulled it off. He took a thick roll of gauze and prepared to wrap my wrist.

"Let Bosco do it," I said.

Bosco obliged, and he had a much gentler touch.

"You make a good nurse," I told him.

"I was part of an ambulance crew in the war."

"No kidding? How'd you end up becoming a comedian?"

"Who can afford medical school? Besides, I was always a comedian."

Mayhew found three glasses and filled them all about half-full. "If you gentlemen don't mind my sharing a drink with you, I'm a bit done up. What exactly happened tonight, Mr. Hatchett?"

I told my tale. I described the wire that had been stretched along the stairs. I mentioned the strange noise I had investigated, and the arrow whizzing by my valuable neck. Bosco and Mayhew were properly impressed.

"But I saved the damned flashlight," I told

them. "I must have been clutching it in my right hand while I tumbled down the steps. My wrist must have taken most of the abuse."

"What a harrowing last few hours you've had, sir. Perhaps we should recruit Cam to help you on your night vigils."

"I prefer to work alone. Don't bother Cam. I could use a bigger gun, though. My wrist won't let me hang on to a shotgun very well, but it will look scary if anybody's watching. Are there any firearms in the manor? I didn't see any worth bothering with in the trophy room."

"The firearms are kept in the gun room, sir."

"Gun room, huh? I hope it's kept locked up."

"Yes indeed, sir."

"It may not matter. Someone around here has managed to get ahold of some keys."

"I take mine to bed with me, sir. And I understand Simone does the same."

"Well, somebody was able to get into the trophy room the night I was sapped. Any part-time burglars on the staff?"

"Not that I'm aware of, sir."

"Maybe we'll be finding out, if I ever track down who's pulling these stunts. Lead me to the gun room, Mayhew, if you don't mind."

Mayhew took us to a room about two doors down from the trophy room. The door was made out of steel with nubby rivets all over it. It had two locks and Mayhew unlocked both of them. He swung the door open and we stepped inside.

There was a huge fireplace, but it wasn't lit like all the others in the house. The room was cold. On the walls were several gun racks, interspersed with trophy heads of big moose, elk, antelope and deer. There were even a couple of bear heads, jaws opened menacingly, and an entire stuffed mountain lion in a glass case in one corner. There were also several manikins dressed in ancient-looking suits of armor.

I looked over the shotguns first. I found a swell old Parker double barreled twelve-gauge. It was a beauty. Nothing but class. Some kind of curly grained walnut stock, with fancy checkering, and lots of silver trim and engraving on the receiver and barrel. I fell in love with it.

"Mind if I borrow this one?" I asked Mayhew, hefting the big gun in my hands. It hurt my wrist a little to hold it, but I was hoping my wrist would be better before my next round of guard duty began.

"Certainly, sir. That was one of Mr. Waldrous' favorites."

"You have shells?"

"Of course, sir. What size shot would you prefer?"

"I doubt if you have buckshot. Number fours will do."

He unlocked a wooden cabinet and sorted through boxes of shells until he found a half-full box of what I'd asked for. I took a handful of shells and put them in my pockets. Bosco was looking over the armor.

"You think you'd like wearing one of those tin cans instead of your jester's outfits?" I asked him.

"Brother, I'd be willing to try it."

I started looking over the iron apparel myself. One manikin was wearing some kind of chain mail shirt or tunic. On its wooden head it wore a hood also made of chain mail. It was a bit rusty but looked to be in pretty good shape.

"What say I borrow this too, Mayhew?"

"Armor, sir? If you wish. But please be careful with it."

"Why, is it dry clean only? I'm going to try it on." I worked the shirt and hood off the dummy and put them both on over Waldrous's Oxford shirt. The hood fit fine but the tunic was a bit tight around the shoulders and too snug around the middle. But beggars can't be choosers. "I want a knife too. Are there any in here?"

"No, sir. We'll have to go to the trophy room."

We headed that way. When we got there I noticed that the door was slightly ajar. I hadn't notice it when we'd gone by the room before, but I wasn't really looking. Mayhew was distressed.

"I'm certain I closed and locked this door last night," he said.

We went in. Damned if there weren't a lot of weapons missing. You could see where they'd hung on the walls. Mostly knives and swords, but also axes, a bow and a quiver of arrows, and a couple of spears. Mayhew looked as close to angry as I'd ever seen him. "This won't do, it won't do. Someone's been pillaging weapons."

"I don't suppose you can blame them," I said. "Things are pretty scary around here."

"I'll have to search the servant's rooms," said Mayhew. "And could I ask one of you gentlemen to search Mr. Cotton's room, and Miss Ursula's?"

"I'll do it," said Bosco. "I don't mind going through Ursula's closet. I wonder what she's got in the way of nighties besides what she was filling out so nicely a little while ago."

I took a gander at the picked-over knives. I found a nice curvy-bladed thing that the tag under it said was a Jambiya. It had a wooden sheath. My mail shirt came with a mail belt you could tie around it and I stuck the Jambiya in the front of it. I felt pretty safe. Pretty spiffy, too.

"Thanks for all your help, Mayhew," I told him. "I appreciate it."

"I'm very concerned for your health, sir."

"Say, Mayhew," said Bosco, "as long as we're here, how would it be if I borrowed one of these swords? I mean, everybody else in the house is armed."

Mayhew frowned, thought it over. "Perhaps a knife from the kitchen, Mr. Bosco."

"What, a little paring knife or something? What good is that? I'm thinking more of something like this Spartan short sword."

Mayhew sighed. "I suppose, but be careful with it. Don't play with it at the dining table. And don't use it as a source of levity."

"Wouldn't think of it."

I looked at my watch. It was getting close to three o'clock. "I've got to be getting back to my bed. Sorry to spoil the party, but I need to get some shut-eye before breakfast."

"Absolutely, sir." Said Mayhew.

"Sweet dreams," said Bosco.

I got back to my room. The first thing I did was to look in my closet and along the walls to make sure there was no access to the servants' passages. That done, I removed my armor and other clothes and got into bed.

Of course I couldn't sleep at first. Too much to think about. It had occurred to me at some point that I was likely dealing with two would-be killers instead of one. When I'd heard the strange noise in the great room, or wherever, and had gone to investigate it, whoever had made the sounds could have doubled back and slipped past me and waited in a doorway until I'd come back to my room. Then they could have shot the arrow when my back was turned.

Of course, that could have been kind of risky. There was a chance I might spot the person when I was shining my flashlight around. But if there'd been two people, working together, the noise-maker in the great room could have hidden someplace before I even got there. And the second person could have been hiding someplace safe until I came back. Two murderers are a whole lot worse than one.

I tried to think of what two people in the house were likely to pair off. Paddy and Ursula? Mayhew and Abigail? Bosco and Mavis? Cam and his secret wife, or whoever it was I'd heard making noise in the carriage house? Mary Elizabeth and Simone? The last pair seemed the most unlikely. Simone hated the little princess. Or maybe she was just pretending? I hadn't been around Cam enough to even guess what he might do.

Mayhew and Abigail seemed unlikely killers. Mayhew showed true devotion to Dunty and Cleo, and Abigail was eternally in their debt, at least as she saw it. And I'd learned to like Bosco, though of course that was a lousy reason to not suspect him.

Paddy and Ursula made sense. Paddy was wanting money badly. Ursula seemed completely his slave. But how could I prove it? I had no real evidence.

Things weren't going the way I wanted them to. I needed to start doing some real investigating, and doing some better thinking than I'd done so far.

I finally fell asleep. A deep and dreamless sleep. Mayhew's scratching at my door woke me at about six-thirty. When I opened the door he had a tea kettle of hot water for me, to wash up and shave with.

"Good morning, sir. Did you sleep well?"

"Like the dead. I'm hungry. Let me get washed

up and dressed and I'll head for the dining room."

"Very good, sir."

"And do something for me, will you? Pick out some nice clothes of Waldrous's for me to wear. You're a class guy. You know how to match up colors and all that."

"I'd be delighted, sir."

While I sponged off, shaved, smeared some pomade on my hair, and rinsed the whiskey out of my mouth, Mayhew selected clothes and laid them out on the bed. I put on tan linen pants with a knife-edge crease, a pale green silk shirt and a darker green necktie, tan silk socks, a pair of ostrich leather loafers, and a loose-fitting off-white linen jacket. I checked myself out in the mirror. I didn't know I could look so good. I wanted to make a good impression this morning. I didn't like that probably half the household thought I was a boozer. I was ready to charm and delight. And I was hungry.

I was the last one at table. Dirk was already piling food onto his plate though everyone else was waiting for me. Ursula gave me an admiring smile. Even Mavis and Mary Elizabeth cooed under their breath when they passed behind my chair. Paddy looked envious, and Cleo and Dunty were all smiles. And when Bosco made a joke about the way I was dressed, nobody laughed. I'd always heard that clothes make the man, but I'd never believed it before.

I was satisfied to see Dirk had a puffy scuff on

his chin. He fingered his jaw a couple of times when he thought I wasn't looking. Everybody else was in a good mood, and why not? The storm was over. The sun was out. Typical Colorado. Maybe Cam could take the Buick out today and drive to the Utilities building, and the phone company. Maybe the water pipes would thaw out and, if we were lucky, they wouldn't have burst. A great day.

Bosco told some terrible jokes and I almost laughed at some of them. He was more than usually talkative this morning.

"I got to see your gun room today," he told Dunty. "Axe was picking out a shotgun. I think he's going pheasant hunting tonight. That's some swell room. I never knew you hunted."

"I don't anymore," said Dunty. He looked almost rosy-cheeked. "But as a boy and young man I often went. Waldrous and I hunted a great deal."

"Yeah?" said Bosco. "Anybody else at this table hunt?"

"I'm an elk hunter," said Dirk, in his self-satisfied croak.

"Really?" I asked, turning to him. "Do you shoot them or just sneak up on them and strangle them with those oh-so-strong hands?"

"Shut up, window peeper."

"I'm more of a fisherman myself," said Paddy. "Though I have shot carp with a bow and arrow."

As soon as he said it he got a shocked look on his face, but the cat was out of the bag: Paddy could shoot a bow and arrow. Nobody said anything, and their silence was telling.

"Well, when you shoot fish they're only a few feet away," said Paddy. "Anybody could do it." He concentrated on his eggs and bacon for the rest of the meal.

I felt pretty happy. Paddy could have shot that arrow last night. He'd had the servants' door in his room unblocked. He could have sneaked around in the secret passageways and set up the booby trap that almost killed me. He could have sapped me. He wanted money badly. If he could kill Dunty, he might come into a nice piece of change. And if that didn't work out, he could probably sweet-talk Cleo into loaning him money. Ursula was devoted to him and would do anything he asked her to. It was all fitting together nicely.

"How are you feeling this morning, Mr. Hatchett?" Cleo asked me. "You had quite an awful night."

"Awful is the right word. But I'm as chipper as a chipmunk and as hungry as a baby hippo this morning."

I ate some of everything except for the kidney pie. I even out-ate Dirk, and that's saying something.

"Mayhew has given us good news," said Dunty. "He talked to Cam when Cam was plowing snow early this morning. Cam's going to take the Buick out today and see if some of our services can be restored. And the water pipes are unthawing. The taps are beginning to drip. Soon everything will be back to normal. Except, of course, for those most unfortunate death threats against me. But soon we'll be able to call in the police. Perhaps today. I'm confident they can help us with the situation. Soon the scoundrel who threatened me and killed my brother will be behind bars."

I hoped he was right, but I didn't believe it. We were still a long ways from apprehending the so-called murderer. Even if it turned out to be Paddy, we'd have to collect a lot more evidence before his guilt could be proven.

That thought soured my temper a little. I decided to take a walk outside. Mayhew was kind enough to bring me one of Waldrous's fur overcoats, and a brown homburg a lot nicer than my fedora. I could almost learn to like this dressing-up business.

11

I decided to walk down to the carriage house and check up on Cam. I hoped he hadn't left in the Buick yet. I soon saw him sawing up an old dead tree that had come down in the storm. Come to think of it, we'd used up a lot of firewood in the last couple of days; he must have been doing a lot of sawing. Cam put down his bow saw when he spied me coming and walked out to meet me.

"You scared me," he said. "In them clothes I thought it was old Waldrous for a moment, come back to life. You're doing OK I see."

"Couldn't be better, except for a few aches and pains. I don't suppose you've got a cup of coffee handy in the house, do you?"

He gave me a wide-eyed look. "I can make some for you. It'll take a while. You stay out here and I'll go make it. If you want to warm yourself, saw some wood."

"Why can't I just come inside with you?"

"Place is a mess. You wouldn't like it."

"I don't mind. I'm only dressed fancy; I don't mind a little clutter."

"But I don't want you seeing the place." He high-tailed it into the house and slammed the door. I even heard him bolt it shut. Come on, Cam, I thought, introduce me to your wife, or whoever you have in there.

I would have sawed up some wood while I waited, but I didn't want to spoil Waldrous's clothes. I walked around the house and tried to peek into windows, but there weren't many on the ground floor and the shades were pulled. In a few minutes Cam opened the door and beckoned me in.

"Just needed to straighten up the place a little," he explained, once I was inside.

He must have been hell on wheels with a dust mop and broom, I thought. The place was immaculate. He offered me a mug of steaming coffee and I drank it down gratefully. I decided to use the direct approach.

"Who you got hiding upstairs, Cam? Is it your wife? Somebody told me you had one."

"Who told you such a thing?"

"I don't remember. It doesn't matter, does it? Why you keeping her secret?"

"What I got upstairs the old woman may not like."

"No? What business is it of hers if you're married or not? It's a free country."

"The old man already knows my secret. He

didn't know what to think. He said I'd have to give him some time. I keep waiting to be fired. He said he wouldn't tell the old woman until he thought things through."

"He can't forbid his employees to marry. That's ridiculous."

"It's not what you think, I don't care who you talked to. It's just something I need to keep private."

"Oh, I see. So Dunty's found out your secret, whatever it is. And if he tells Cleo she might want to fire you. Why, what're you hiding? Two wives? I guess if the old man kicked off about now you'd have a better chance of keeping your position. Tell your wife to come on down, I won't eat her. Is she a looker?"

"I ain't talking to you about it. Think whatever you want. And forget about my wanting to knock off the old man. It ain't true."

"Sure, I believe you. Has Mayhew or anyone told you about some of the excitement we've been having in the big house?"

"He told me some things this morning. I'm glad I'm not living there. The old man will be dead of a heart attack if something's not done soon."

"I'm trying my best, believe me. I think I may have a suspect, but I'll keep that under my hat for now."

"Is it that Dirk fellow?"

"Any particular reason you think it might be?"

"I don't care for the mug. I hear tell he was

kicked off the police force, and he pushes his way around too much. Now, you think on it. Dirk had things pretty easy when he was watching the old man's brother. Good chow, cute maids to flirt with, everything nice and comfortable. And then Waldrous gets his head cut off and Dirk's out of work again. Now he's back. Get the connection? What if it's him that's been mailing threatening letters and gray wigs and all? You see, he's got his cushy job back. Something to think on."

"He'd only have a job as long as Dunty lives. And the old man was almost scared to death last night. Dirk might not be fool enough to go shooting arrows, or letting off banshee screams at two o'clock in the morning."

"He don't strike me as a smart one, that Dirk."

"I'm inclined to agree. Say, I heard something about you maybe taking the Buick out this morning and talking to the phone company and the utilities company."

"Sure, that's what I'm going to do. The streets should be plowed most places now. I'll look for a pay phone, though, so I don't have to do more driving than I have to. You need something? Pack of cigarettes or something?"

"No, I just need a phone. Maybe I could ride with you."

"Not unless you're in a big hurry for that phone. You got work to do here, don't you?"

"Not that much to do in the daytime. I'm the nightshift guy. Listen, it could take days before the phone and utilities guys can get around to restoring the Flinders' service."

"Naw, they'll do it today. The Flinders family has all kinds of pull in this town. Believe me, I've seen plenty of examples of it."

"I didn't think about that. OK, I guess I'll get going now. Tell the missus I said hello."

"Smart guy, ain't you?"

"Sure, for now."

I thanked him for the coffee and walked back to the manor. Since I was already outside, I made a trip to the private crypts to say a prayer, then I went back into the house. I went up to my room to change into something a little less flashy. However, Mavis and Mary Elizabeth were cleaning my room: changing the sheets, sweeping the rug, refilling my pitcher.

"We'll be done in a minute, Mr. Hatchett," said Mary Elizabeth.

"Take your time, I'm in no hurry. You girls work well together."

"Yeah, we're a good team," said Mavis.

"Did you play baseball in school too, Mavis?"

"Not me. I was track and field, if you can believe." She laughed. "Wasn't it a riot when Mr. Cotton told everybody about how he'd shot fish in a barrel with a bow and arrow?"

"Fish in a lake, or a stream," said Mary Elizabeth. "Not a barrel."

"Same difference. I thought he was going to croak from thinking folks would blame him for shooting off that arrow last night."

"It couldn't have been him," said Mary Elizabeth. "He's not that sort."

"Oh, yeah? You're just stuck on him."

"He's very handsome."

"He ain't aging well."

"He looks very distinguished."

"Right. I'm sure Methuselah looked distinguished too." Mavis put a hand on one curvy hip and rolled her eyes.

"Anybody could have shot that arrow."

"Wrong, honey. It's not easy. You should try it sometime."

"I'll stick with baseball."

"Better keep that bat handy by your bed, I think Dirk's been giving you the eye."

"That's horrid. He's disgusting." Mary Elizabeth wrinkled her comely nose and wiped her palms on her lacy apron.

"Oh? Don't you think he's distinguished looking?"

"No, and I'm glad Mr. Hatchett hit him."

"I would have hit him harder if my right wrist had been working," I said.

"That was so awful what happened to you," said Mary Elizabeth. "Getting tripped up on the stairs and all. You could have broken your neck."

"Yeah. Maybe that will happen tonight."

"I hope we have electricity by then. I think we're finished, Mr. Hatchett."

The girls left my room, still chattering at each

other. I looked through the closet to find something inelegant to wear. I was tired of being a well-dressed man; it gave people false hopes. I didn't have much luck. No dungarees and work shirts. I finally found a pair of plain cotton pants and a cotton dress shirt. Waldrous's slumming outfit, maybe. I changed, including putting my own shoes back on. Dammed if Mayhew or somebody hadn't polished them!

I thought about Mavis. Track and field? Running, hurdling, pole vaulting, broad jumping — emphasis on the broad — maybe shot putting and javelin throwing. She must have been pretty athletic in her day. And it sounded like she had some experience with a bow and arrow. I wondered if Mavis and Mary Elizabeth were the partners in crime who'd been terrorizing the inhabitants of the manor and threatening Dunty. Impossible to say. I went out to the great room.

Dunty and Cleo were there, sitting by the fire. The old woman was sewing little bells on that damned jester's uniform she was making for Bosco. The old man was smoking his pipe and sipping at a glass of brandy. Dirk was standing at a window looking at the slowly-melting snow drop in great slushy lumps from the tree branches.

I took a seat, uninvited, and got ready to grill the old couple about a few things I'd thought up. My chair was sitting sideways to the fire. Dunty and Cleo's chairs were facing the fire. While I sat there, Bosco sneaked out from somewhere and came up behind Dunty. He had a paper bag in his hand that he'd blown air into. I couldn't believe he was going to do what I thought he was going to do.

When he was standing right behind the old man's chair he raised the bag with one hand and slapped it hard with his other. I just sat there like a dumb shamus. The bursting bag made a noise like a big fat firecracker going off. Dunty jumped a foot and clawed at his heart. He turned blue. Damn that Bosco. The idiot began laughing, but not for long. Cleo lit into him.

"How dare you, Bosco! How dare you! You could have killed my husband. Go to your room, and don't bother coming out for luncheon."

Dunty had got ahold of himself by now, but he was mad.

"Why must we continue to employ that insufferable clown, Cleo? Why not get a television like other people?"

"You know I find it offensive. Besides, Bosco didn't mean any harm. He's just like a little boy, you know that."

"One of these days I'll give him his walking papers, with or without your approval."

I decided this wasn't a good time to grill the Flinders. Dirk had jumped and turned around when Bosco had popped his bag. Now he stood glaring at me like he thought I had something to do with it.

"Mr. Flinders," I said, "would you mind if I

went into the library and purloined one of your fine Cubans?'

"Help yourself, son, help yourself."

"Thanks"

"Keep away from the brandy," Dirk snarled at me while I was leaving the room. I decided to let remark fall on deaf ears.

I went into the library, lit up a cigar, and stood in front of the fire, thinking. Maybe I'd been wrong about Bosco. He might not be such a good guy after all. That paper bag trick could have given old Flinders a fatal heart attack. I remembered that Bosco had tried to make me believe Paddy was the would-be killer. He might have been deflecting suspicion away from himself.

But was Mavis his partner? Or Simone? Or even Dirk? Bosco seemed to have the run of the house. And it was possible he could have found a chance to have the household keys duplicated at some point. As for his following me around in a comradely fashion, maybe he was just keeping an eye on me.

I heard a noise of trucks and looked out the library window. Cam had been right — the Flinders family still had a lot of pull in Quartz Quarry. Cam must have found a phone. A big yellow utilities truck had pulled up the broad walk in front of the house. I saw Mayhew out front talking to a guy in a winter coat and a ball cap. It looked like we might have electricity pretty soon. The truck had a cherry picker on it, and pretty soon a guy was in the bucket trimming away tree branches.

While I was watching him, a white van from the telephone company showed up. Things were moving in a hurry. We'd be back in the twentieth century in no time at all. I strolled out to the front entry way, pulled on my coat and hat and stepped outside to have a word with Mayhew. He was still giving instructions to the workmen.

"Looks like we'll be fixed up pretty soon," I greeted him.

"Yes, sir, and won't it be a blessing. As soon as Cam returns we can start cutting up some of these fallen branches for firewood. I'm afraid we're running low. Mr. Dunty always likes a fire, even in warm weather. I do hope Cam has contacted the police."

"Oh, yeah. Them. I suppose they'll have to investigate what's been happening around here the last couple of days."

"Indeed, and perhaps they can provide additional security for Mr. Dunty. Of course, sir, I'm not questioning your own capable handling of the situation, or Mr. Dirk's. But the more the merrier, as they say."

"Sure. Nothing like a bunch of cops around to make a guy merry."

I went back into the house in a foul mood. I just wanted a phone not cops. I went back to the great room; Dunty, Cleo and Dirk were still there.

I spoke directly to Dunty. "I guess the police will be arriving soon. What are you going to tell them?" I paused. "I hope you aren't going to insist that whoever's threatening you is an outsider."

"But I'm sure that's the case," said Cleo. "I don't know why you think otherwise."

"How would they get in at night? How could they ramble through the whole house without anybody seeing them? It's an inside job, I'm certain."

"Yeah, so who's the killer then?" asked Dirk. "One of the maids? The old cook?"

"I don't know yet, but I'll find out. Some of your old play fellows, the cops, will be dropping by later, Dirk. You looking forward to seeing your old friends, or are they still sore at you?"

"I've still got friends on the force."

"Have you now? I'd hate to meet those friends."

Speaking of the devil, right then I heard the front door open, and in a moment Mayhew appeared leading a couple of uniformed cops and a lanky, cadaverous-looking guy in a brown suit and unbuttoned overcoat.

"The police," Mayhew said to Dunty. "Wanting to see you, sir."

I was glad Bosco wasn't present. These guys looked like they were in sour moods. His jokes likely wouldn't be well-received.

"You may speak in front of my wife, my bodyguard, and my detective," Dunty told the guy in the suit. "Mayhew, bring tea for the gentlemen."

Boy, that got them excited. Tea! Just what they wanted, no doubt. The lanky guy sat down in a chair facing Dunty and Cleo. The uniformed cops remained standing. I looked at them, and damned if I didn't recognize one of them. Officer Biff Munson. I'd made his acquaintance a while back when he'd been sent with another cop to investigate a near murder I'd found myself in the middle of. I sidled over to him.

"Hey, Biff. How's the flat feet? How's Marge?" Marge was Officer Ringo, Biff's little sweetheart.

"Axe, old buddy. How's the gumshoe game? Marge is swell. We're talking about getting hitched."

"That so? I'm thinking along the same lines myself. In fact, I've popped the question already."

"And she said yes?"

"Sure. There's no accounting for taste."

Biff looked at his superior, who was busy annoying the Flinders, then backed up a ways and gestured with his head for me to join him. I walked over and stood beside him.

"So what's the scoop?" Biff asked, in a whisper.

"Damned if I know. You remember a guy getting his head cut off in this place a few months ago?"

"Sure, I know something about it. But I had nothing to do with that case. This is my first trip to the manor. Didn't that case involve some kind of fake beard and mustache or something? Something crazy like that?"

"A gray toupee. This guy's brother," I nodded my head at Dunty, "got a gray toupee in the mail, and some threatening letters, and a little later he got murdered in his bed. Right here in the mansion. Then, a few days ago, Mr. Flinders here gets a letter and a gray toupee of his own in the mail. I don't know who killed his brother, some outsider. But I'd bet money what's going on now is an inside job. One of the servants or guests. I don't have a handle on it yet."

"Keeping busy? What's that bum Dirk doing here? Arranging for another Flinders to get bumped off?"

"Too busy drinking and stuffing his flabby gut. You guys on the force must miss him."

"Like a boil on our patooties."

I gave him a brief rundown of what'd happened to me in the last couple of days or so. Biff gave a low whistle, not too loud.

"You got to watch that stuff. Saps and booby traps and flying arrows. A guy's got to look out for his health."

"I'll be damned careful tonight, you can count on it."

"The lieutenant's going to want to talk to everybody in the house. And guess what? Me, I'm staying. I got my little overnight bag packed. Marge sent along some sandwiches she made. Swell, huh?"

"You'll be a welcome addition. Really. And you won't need those sandwiches. Abigail, the cook, puts on a good spread."

Dunty rang his bell, and a moment later Mayhew appeared. A butler's life is waiting for bells to be rung.

"Mayhew," Dunty addressed him, "round up the servants and guests. The lieutenant here will want to speak to them. Gather everyone in the library. Send Bosco to fetch Cam."

"I've confined Bosco to his room," protested Cleo.

"Yes, dear, but we need him now. Mayhew will see to it that Bosco returns to his room after he's summoned Cam and has been questioned by the lieutenant."

12

I waited around while folks gathered. When Paddy and Ursula showed up I made my move. I figured their doors would be locked and I didn't want to bother with picking the locks, so I headed for the servant's passage. I fumbled around with my flashlight and tried to find the little door that would take me into Paddy's room. I tried a couple of doors that were blocked before I found the one that opened into his room. It pushed open easily enough.

When I got inside I saw that two big trunks, stacked one on top of the other, had been pushed up against the door. I took a look in the top one and it was empty. I swung his closet door open. There were a bunch of bricks, rocks, old telephone books, even a couple of fireplace logs on the floor. The former contents of the emptied trunks.

I didn't know exactly what I was looking for. A spool of wire, a bow. I found neither, but in a dresser drawer I found a big knife with an African look to it. I ducked back into the servants' passage and moved along to Ursula's room.

The little servant's door that led into her room was easy to open. More empty trunks. I looked in her closet. My god the dame had a lot of clothes. And plenty of frilly bedroom attire. Paddy was a lucky man. Under her bed I found a slim dagger and a tomahawk. Bosco had said he would check Paddy and Ursula's bedrooms and collect the weapons from the trophy room he found. Maybe he'd changed his mind. Everybody needed protection in a place like this.

I tried some of the other doors along the passageway, but all of them were blocked. I went out to my room, dusted myself off a bit, and went back to the great room. No one was there. Poor old Axe was alone.

I went to the window and watched the phone and utilities guys working. They were making a lot of noise. Cutting tree limbs, shouting, having a great time. I went into the kitchen and tried turning on the water. It ran some rust for a while then came out clean and strong. At least that was fixed. I hoped none of the pipes had burst. I sat down in a chair and rested my tired feet.

Who was after Dunty? Did they really hope to scare him to death? I didn't think that would work. He'd had some pretty big shocks in the last couple of days and his heart was still ticking. I wondered why Cam hadn't been asked to call a doctor when he was out. Maybe Dunty's heart condition wasn't as bad as he made out. Maybe he just liked drinking brandy and smoking a pipe.

While I was sitting and thinking, the electricity came back on. Lights went on everywhere. I heard the furnace growl to life somewhere in the cellar. I got up and checked the phone that sat on a little table not far from the fireplace. There was no dial tone. I thought of sneaking off to the library, standing outside the door, eavesdropping. It seemed like a pretty good idea, so I put it into action.

Biff was standing guard outside the open library door.

"How are things going?" I asked him.

He gave a big shrug. "I don't know, I can't hardly hear nothing. There's a dame in there with a voice like a buzz saw cutting through barb wire."

"That would be Simone, the housekeeper."

"What's she do in her spare time, sing in the choir?"

"Let's hope not. So what do they want you to do around here — stand guard over Dunty?"

"Is that the old man?"

"Yeah."

"Funny name. I don't know what they got planned for me. I'd vote for drinking beer."

"You might have to settle for wine, or whiskey, or brandy."

"I could suffer through it. That Dirk guy gets on my nerves. I never could stand him when he was on the force. You like the guy?"

"You notice the bump on his chin?"

"Yeah. How'd he get it?"

"I put it there."

"Good for you! I'm liking you more all the time. Who's the little guy in the clown suit?"

"Bosco. He's their resident Milton Berle."

"Who's the tall blonde with all the curves going every which way?"

"Ursula. She's a secretary."

"That so? I've got some dictation for her."

"Forget it. She belongs to Paddy Cotton, the silver-haired dream boat."

"That guy? He's too old for her. But what do I care? I got Marge."

"That's the way to talk. I wish they'd get the damned phones fixed so I can put in a call to my girl. I hope the snow treated her right. Say, what's going on in there? Has your lieutenant let anybody out yet?"

"Naw. He's keeping everybody. I don't figure it somehow."

"Think he'll want to talk to me?"

"Sure he will. He wants to talk to everybody. For a guy who ain't friendly, he talks a lot. Even to folks on the street he wouldn't know from Adam."

"Who's Adam?"

"Funny guy."

"Maybe I should go in. I mean, if he's going to talk to me anyhow. What are you doing guarding the room ? There's nobody out here but me and you. I'm going inside."

"Nosey peeper."

"I could say something about nosey flatfoots with eyes for fleshy curves."

"Go in, see if I care. But if I get in trouble — "

"It won't happen. Here goes nothing."

I went into the library. Everybody belonging to the house was sitting on chairs and couches on the fireplace side of the room, except for Simone. It must be her turn with the lieutenant.

At the other end of the room they'd set up a screen, an old thing Mayhew must have dug out of the attic, designed to keep drafts off of you. It was set up in front of a long library table, so the cop in charge could have some privacy while he grilled his victims. The other uniformed cop, a guy too small for such work, was standing importantly on our side of the screen trying not to make eye contact with anyone.

I took a seat with the others. Some of them were talking in whispers. I sat next to Mayhew and Abigail.

"What gives?" I asked the butler. "They're not letting any of you out."

"No, sir. It's inconvenient. We have a household to run. Perhaps the lieutenant is hoping one of the persons being questioned will reveal something about one of the others. Then he'll have the monster handy to arrest."

"There's an idea. You might be right. I guess I'll take my turn with the others. How many to go?"

"Only Mr. Bosco, sir."

I looked around. Even Dunty and Cleo were here, in their own quiet corner. Cleo was stitching on that damned outfit of Bosco's. She must have forgiven him. Dunty was looking over a stack of newspapers that Cam must have bought for him in town. Cam was standing over in a corner, with his back to the wall, like he wasn't too happy about the crowd.

In a minute Simone made her appearance, looking more severe and unhappy than ever. Then the lieutenant ducked his head around the screen. "Next." That was Bosco's cue. The little jester squirmed in his chair a second and then bearded the lion. He passed me by without even looking at me. He went around the screen and I heard him laugh. What was the guy doing, making fun of the lieutenant's clothes? He didn't have a lot of sense.

Bosco was on the rack for about ten minutes. When he came out he looked scorched. Lieutenant Brown Suit stuck his head back out. "Next."

Mayhew cleared his throat. "There are no others, sir."

The lieutenant came out from behind the screen. He was still wearing his hat, and damned if he wasn't smoking one of Dunty's Cuban cigars.

"All you fine folks can get on with your business," he said, in a booming voice. He saw me. "Shamus, stick around."

"Did you wish to talk to me and my wife any further?" Dunty asked.

"No. All I've got to talk about is police business, and that ain't your business."

I thought both Dunty and Cleo looked a little huffy over that remark, and I couldn't blame them. The room emptied in a hurry. Pretty soon it was just me and the two law-and-order boys.

"Name." The lieutenant shot at me.

"Axel Hatchett, private investigator."

"I've heard of you. You like to stick your nose where it doesn't belong."

"It's where it belongs right now, on my face."

"Don't be disrespectful. You think murder's funny?"

"I kind of get a charge out of Jack the Ripper."

He sighed and his shoulders sagged a little. He wasn't going to scare me and he looked too tired to go on trying.

"What's your take on this situation? Sounds like you've been roughed up some the last couple of days."

"I feel like a boxer who's just thrown five or six fights. I keep taking hits but it's getting me nowhere."

"No ideas? No pet suspects?"

"Not really. It's an inside job, I'm sure of that much."

"Wouldn't take a genius to figure that out. You take care of the old man, you understand? We can't have another Flinders killed in this town."

"No, it wouldn't make you look too good, would it? I'll do my best to keep the old geezer breathing."

"It ought to be simple enough. You'll have Officer Munson to help you and," he made a face, "former officer Drebber, whatever he'll be worth."

"I hope you grilled him good. He's been rubbing his slime on me since the moment I walked into the house."

"I wasn't easy on him. Listen, Hatchett, I hear your phones will be back in order pretty soon. Don't forget to call us if anything comes up. Anything."

"If anything comes up, you and the boys will be the first to know."

"Good. Now go about your business."

That was swell with me. I left the library and drifted out to the great room. Cleo, Dunty and Dirk again. I heard a clashing of cutlery in the dining room. No doubt the servants were busting their humps trying to get lunch on the table on time. There was an hour to go, but they'd all been interrupted.

"What did you think of our lieutenant?" Dunty asked me.

"A very commanding presence, but his shoes could use a polish."

"I noticed that too," said Cleo, affably. "And he kept his hat on in the house." She didn't like the guy.

I wandered over to a chair and sat down. Then the phone rang. The phone rang! I immediately went off looking for Mayhew. I found him in the kitchen, talking to Abigail.

"Mayhew, could I borrow one of your phones? I've got an important call to make."

"Certainly, sir. Why not use the telephone in Mr. Dunty's office?"

"Thanks, I will."

"Sir, I've given Officer Munson the bedroom next to yours."

"That'll be great."

I went to Dunty's office and helped myself to the phone. I called Rocko's but couldn't get a connection. Their phone must be out of order. I guess Rocko didn't have the kind of pull the Flinders had. Tracy lived above Rocko's and didn't even have a phone. I decided to call her parents' restaurant, Jeremiah's Wild Game Grubbery, but I didn't know the number.

I looked around the office, hunting for a phone book. It was a swell place with its big desk, built-in bookcases, and nice wood filing cabinets. I wondered why Dunty didn't keep it locked up. All of his important papers would be in here. The filing cabinets were antiques with locks you could pick with your thumbnail.

I thought about Paddy and Ursula being in here typing up some of Paddy's manuscript. It would have been a good opportunity for Paddy to go through Dunty's papers, maybe get a gander at how the old man's business deals were coming along. He likely had a safe in here too. I thought about the fact that whoever our would-be killer was may have jimmied the lock on the trophy room door.

I started looking for a safe. I looked behind a big gilt-framed painting of Flinty Flinders himself that hung on the wall behind the desk. No luck. There was a picture of an overweight horse on one wall. I went to move it and it swung out on a hinge on one side. Eureka! The safe. It was the kind you lock with a key rather than a combination.

I took a close gander at it. It had a baked-on green finish. And there were some tiny scratches around the lock like somebody had been fiddling at it with a pick. I checked the filing cabinets and they too had scratches around the locks. Somebody in the house was desperate for money, or information. I had a feeling it was Paddy Cotton.

I found a phone book in a desk drawer and called Jeremiah's. Their phone worked. After a few rings a pleasant-sounding woman came on the line.

"Jeremiah's. Are you hankering for a wild game meal at our grubbery?"

"Not at the moment. Is this Mrs. Clover?"

"Sure is. Who's this?"

"Axe Hatchett, your daughter's fiancé."

"Sure. I bet you've been trying to call her. Right, honey?"

"You bet. I don't suppose you've heard from her."

"She called from a payphone a while back.

She's fine, just tired of the snow, and missing you."

"I know the feeling. Listen, Mrs. Clover, if you talk to her again would you have her call me at the Flinders' mansion?" I gave her the number.

"I'll sure do that. You doing all right?"

"In the middle of a case, but, yeah, I'm OK. Thanks a lot. Tell your husband hello for me."

"I will. He'll be happy to have heard from you."

I said goodbye and hung up the phone. Then I left the office and wandered toward the dining room. I ran into Biff hanging around the doorway.

"Sure smells good," he greeted me. "Smells like Thanksgiving in there."

"I told you. Abigail is a cracker-jack cook. Let's go sit down."

We were early, the first ones in the room. I had Biff sit down in Dirk's chair. To hell with the guy. Maybe he could sit on Ursula's lap. Biff and I got to talking.

"Say, I'm going to take a little nappy nap after we eat so I can help you with your prowling to-night."

"Thanks. I might need help. You sure you're up to it?"

"Danger and menace is my middle name."

"That's two names. What do you think of the layout so far?"

"Swank place. Couple of swell skirts."

"How about the murder angle. Have you thought of that at all?"

"Am I here for that?"

Dirk joined us. He frowned at Biff. "That's my chair, Munson."

"Officer Munson to you, pal. This chair's occupied and it's going to stay that way. Maybe you can eat in the kitchen."

13

This pleasant exchange of greetings was interrupted by the entrance of the other diners. Everybody showed up but Bosco. Apparently Cleo had stuck with her idea of keeping him confined to his room. Dunty and Cleo looked less put out than when the lieutenant had been present. Paddy looked like he had aged ten years since breakfast. Even Ursula looked a trifle less divine than usual. I wondered what was up.

Dirk had to pull up a chair from a corner of the room and squeeze it in between me and Biff. He didn't have enough elbow room and it affected his eating. Still, he almost kept up with Biff, an all time champion trencherman.

"Say, what are these little canaries dipped in Jell-O?" Biff asked our hostess.

Cleo drew herself up stiffly.

"I believe those are infant wood pigeons smothered in quince aspic. Are they to your liking, officer?"

"Sure, they're swell. I could eat a dozen."

"You already have," snarled Dirk."

"Look who's talking," said Biff, around a big mouthful of bird. "How many of them bacon-wrapped sausages have you put in your craw?"

"Those are freshwater eels," explained Cleo.

"What? Eels?" Biff made a face and reached for a platter of lamb chops. He anointed them with butter and syrup and sent them down his gullet.

"You took the last chop," Dirk complained. "You're a pure hog, Munson."

"Better than being half hog, half alligator," said Biff. "Shut up and eat your pigeon kidneys."

"They're shrimps, soaked in something, I'm done with them, but I'll take some more of them potatoes and onions. Pass them over, fatty."

"Look who's calling somebody fat. They could melt down your gut and grease a couple of loco-motive engines with the oil." He passed the plate of potatoes to Dirk, but not before helping himself to half of them. "You mind passing down some of them little trout?"

"Fingerling sturgeon," said Cleo, with a heavy sigh.

"Sure, sturgeon," said Biff, forking about half-a-dozen fish onto his already stacked plate. "Mind if I eat the heads and all? Kind of remind me of sardines."

"Anybody want them last five slices of ham?" asked Dirk, sharpening his knife on his fork.

"The maids are happy to serve you," said Cleo.

"You gentlemen needn't act like you're dining in a boarding house."

"Don't want to trouble the help," said Dirk. He rose from his chair and grabbed the platter of ham. Biff stabbed a slice from the plate as it went by him.

"Hey, Blondie. You with the extra curves," said Biff, "you mind sending some of that jelly my direction? Don't bother with that sour orange crap in the — "

"Marmalade," explained Cleo.

"Yeah. Don't bother with that. I'll take the strawberry. I got a couple of biscuits here that needs some lubricating. Thanks."

"Anybody want the rest of them fancy meatballs?" Dirk asked, diving for a bowl.

"I'll take some," said Biff.

"Where you going to put them?" Dirk asked him. "Your plate's full."

"Yeah, but my stomach ain't. You got any ketchup in this place?"

In the midst of this carnage, I ate my meal somewhat absent-mindedly, having plenty of things to think about. Mavis and Mary Elizabeth served as always, neither seeming the worse for wear after their third grilling in the same number of days. Cleo tried making small talk with Biff.

"Did you and Dirk work together on the police force?"

"Was Dirk on the police force? I didn't notice."

"Did you get your orders from Lieutenant Gaspar? About sharing the night shift with Mr. Hatchett?"

"Sure, I got my orders. I'm taking a nap as soon as I've had dessert. What are we having, by the way?"

"I really wouldn't know."

"Sure, you only live here."

"I approve menus weekly. I can't remember what we're having. Maybe some humble pie for you."

"Is that like mincemeat? I don't care for the stuff."

Cleo gave up.

"Mr. Hatchett, I do hope you'll be less reckless tonight than you've been."

"Caution and moderation will be my guides. Actually, I'm looking forward to tonight's festivities. I think I'll catch our criminal."

"Really? Tell us about it."

"No, ma'am, I really can't. I don't want to tip my hand. The murderer might be listening to us right now."

"How horrid. I'm sure that isn't true."

"Time will tell. I've got a pretty good handle on who's been making our night life miserable."

Of course, I really had no kind of handle at all. My money was still on Paddy, but I was a long ways from proving anything. Still, I didn't mind making our would-be killer uncomfortable by pretending I knew more than I did. After dessert — it was pecan caramel pie and Biff had two slices —

he and I headed for our respective bedrooms to get a little beauty sleep while we had the chance. I lay down in my clothes, what the hell, and I was asleep in a surprisingly short time. Mayhew's wakeup call came in time to get me to the dining room before dinner started.

"May I lay out your clothes for you, sir?" Mayhew asked me.

"No, don't bother. I'll find something to throw on."

I put on the same duds I'd worn at lunch and went to the dining room.

Damned if Abigail hadn't made a ragout. I don't know if it was rabbit, but I wasn't trusting it. I whispered to Biff about the infamous nature of our cook's ragouts, but he just shrugged and said his belly could take care of itself. He ate my portion. After dinner, the gentlemen — and me — adjourned to the library and set fire to cigars and drained brandy glasses. I stuck with coffee. So did Biff; he wanted to keep his wits about him.

There was something in the air this evening, an edgy foreboding that I think we all felt. I don't believe in a sixth sense, or intuition, or any of that, but maybe the killer was putting out some special kind of vibrations. The hair on my arms rose up. I was glad when Biff suggested we go on duty early.

"I figure we'll do it this way," Biff said, when we'd reached my guard's chair in the hall. "You sit in the chair for a couple of hours and watch Mr.

Flinders' door, and I'll wander around the house looking for spooks. Then you can hunt for haunts while I sit in the chair. That way we'll both stay fresh. Sound OK to you?"

"I think that's a good plan. You got your revolver with you?"

"On my belt. What, it's too small for you to see? Try looking down the barrel."

"Let me get my own gun," I said, and ducked into my room. I took off my shirt and put on the chain mail one. With no shirt underneath it fit less snug than when I'd tried it on the first time. I pulled the mail hood over my ears and loaded the shotgun and went back out into the hall. Biff gave me a look that was worth looking at.

"Halloween's way over, shamus. What's with the outfit?"

"If you'd been through what I've been through the last couple of nights you'd get an outfit of your own. Trust me."

"Yeah? Where would I find a get-up like that?"

"I got mine in the gun room, but I don't think they have your size."

"This place has a gun room?"

"This place has everything."

"Makes things convenient for the killer."

"I'm afraid that's true. We'll have to be careful."

I spent a couple of hours sitting in my chair, hoping I didn't get an itch where I couldn't scratch it under the chain mail. I'd already shown Biff where the servants' passages were, and acquainted him with the layout of the mansion, and now he was off exploring it. Around ten Mayhew showed up with the silver carafe thing he always put my coffee in.

"Should I have brought two pots, sir? Mr. Biff might want some."

"We can share. At least we won't have to make use of the private crypts, now that the water's back on."

"Yes, sir. We are once again blessed with indoor facilities. The household has retired, sir. Good night. If you need anything, sir, please ring for me."

I drank some coffee. Mayhew had only brought one cup, but Biff and I would manage. By the time two hours had passed I was starting to get sleepy. Biff was late. It was close to midnight when he finally showed up to relieve me. I was happy to trade places with him. I poured him a cup of coffee as he gave my outfit another looking over.

"Watch out for dragons. But if you get a chance to save any damsels in distress, go right ahead."

"Thanks for the marching orders."

I wandered off down the hall. It was a lot less creepy without the flickering candles. So was the hallway where Biff was. I'd set a lamp out on the table in the hall by our guard chair, and there was a second lamp burning on a table farther down the hallway.

When I checked the servants' passage, there were lights to turn on there, too, which was great, but I could hardly keep my eyes open. What the hell? I must be getting old and unable to keep irregular hours.

I checked out the great room, the dining room, and then headed along to the library. It was one o'clock. I opened the door and switched on the light.

I had company: Paddy Cotton. He was lying face-down on the rug, his head facing the door. His limbs were splayed out all over. Some kind of ugly short spear stuck out of his back. A good deal of blood was soaking into the rug.

I bent down and felt for the artery near his throat. There was no pulse. He was as dead as a baked clam. His silvery-gray hair shown in the lamplight. It reminded me of a gray toupee.

Right then I heard the hideous banshee yell I'd heard the night before. I summoned up a yell of my own and raced back to my room. I could only hope that Biff and Dunty were all right. I clutched the shotgun in both hands but I didn't see anything to shoot. I was wide awake by the time I reached Biff. He was asleep in his chair.

Dirk was out in the hall, waving his gun around. Ursula was peeking out her door, her pretty mouth a big "O". Bosco and Cleo stood holding each other, looking at something sticking out of the wall next to Dunty's door. It was a big knife, a dagger, and there was a note attached to it. The servants were piling into the hall now.

"Dirk — where's Dunty," I shouted. "Where's

the old man?"

Dirk and I tried to get into Dunty's room at the same time and wedged ourselves in the doorway. I elbowed him in the ribs for old time's sake, and pushed my way into the room. There was a lamp burning dimly on his nightstand. Dunty was still in bed, his face beneath his nightcap the color of bleached cotton. His eyes were closed and at first I thought he was dead. Then he opened his eyes and said, in a weak whisper: "My pipe. Bring me my pipe, and brandy."

"Thank God you're alive. To hell with your pipe." I checked the windows in his room. They were locked, and I knew that Cam and Bosco had shoveled a couple of tons of snow against them a couple of days ago. I went back out into the hall. "Mr. Flinders is OK," I said, to nobody in particular. I spotted Mayhew. "Call the coppers. Now! Paddy Cotton's been murdered." To one side of me Ursula let out a scream that was fair competition for the banshee yell we'd all heard.

Biff was awake but groggy. He kept blinking his eyes and trying to get out of his chair.

"You've been drugged," I told him. "We both were. Somebody spiked our coffee."

Abigail appeared at my elbow. "It can't be, sir. I made the coffee myself. I didn't put anything in it."

"I'm not saying you did. But somebody put sleeping pills or something into that carafe. Until a minute ago I was half asleep myself. Let's not all bunch up in the hall like this. Go to your rooms and get dressed. The cops will be here soon. Everybody meet in the great room."

"Do as he says," commanded Cleo. "And someone get my husband his pills and other medicines. Hurry!"

I helped Biff out of his chair. "Come on, partner, let's walk." I guided him down the hall and into the great room. I kept walking him up and down until his legs became a little less rubbery.

"Get me some whiskey," he said.

"It'll put you to sleep again."

"No it won't, honest."

I found the brandy decanter and handed it to him. He drank a big gulp of it, and damned if he didn't seem to wake up a little.

"Show me that body," he said.

We went to the library and stood in the doorway staring at the mortal remains of Paddy.

"Jeeze!" said Biff. "I ain't never seen nobody speared before. You sure he ain't still alive?"

"I checked. He's dead all right. I figure that spear must have slipped between a couple of ribs and hit his heart. He didn't die all at once, though. There's too much blood for that. And here I was beginning to believe that Paddy was the guy wanting to murder old man Flinders. There's a dagger with a note on it upstairs, sticking out of the wall next to Dunty's room. I'd like to know what it says, but I left it for the cops to take care of. I don't want to mess up evidence."

In a little bit the doorbell rang and Mayhew answered it. Some cops tramped in. There were two uniformed officers, a guy in civvies holding a camera, and a short man with a too-big hat who I recognized as a homicide mug.

"Coroner's on his way," Big Hat said, though who he was talking to I couldn't have said.

I led the gang to the library. We all stepped in, sidling around the body.

"You find the body?" the homicide guy asked me.

"Yeah, I'm the lucky one."

He turned to his two uniformed cops. "Make sure everybody in the house is rounded up. Don't let anybody even think of leaving."

"They're gathering in the great room," I said. "That's the room off the entry hall you came into."

The two officers nodded and left. Big Hat turned to me again.

"Did you touch the body, move anything? Take anything?"

"Things are just the way I found them."

"I'm Conroy. Homicide."

"Hatchett. Private investigator."

"Haven't I seen you before?"

"I think we might have met at a picnic." He wasn't listening. He was squatted down by the body. The guy with the camera was having a great time taking lots of candid shots of the body and its surroundings. The doorbell rang again. In a minute Mayhew appeared, leading a guy smoking a briar pipe and wearing a wrinkled suit. The coroner.

"He's dead," said the medical authority. "Looks like foul play."

"Quit joking, Aldridge," said Conroy. "Tell me how he died and when."

"The blood on the floor's not even dried yet. I'd say he died recently. Spear in the back makes suicide unlikely. The spear could have been thrown or jabbed into him. One wound. Looks like he crawled a little before he died. Who found him?"

Conroy pointed at me.

"OK, Sir Lancelot, when'd you find him?" I'd forgotten about my chain mail and I'd parked my shotgun by the door. "When'd you find him, crusader?"

"Maybe half an hour ago."

The coroner was untucking Paddy's shirt, pulling it up on his back a ways, looking for lividity. "Naw, guy's been dead longer than that. I'd say he passed through this vale of tears a good hour and a half ago. Who's footprint?" He pointed to a spot on the edge of the blood stain.

"Don't look at me," I said. "I was careful."

"This could make things easy," said Conroy. "Looks like we need to round up some pairs of shoes."

"That's a damned big print," I said. "I don't know if there's anyone in the house who wears shoes that size. Wait a minute. Biff."

"Officer Munson?" asked Conroy. "Where is

the big goof?"

"In the great room."

"Fetch him. And tell him to bring his shoes in his hands."

I went out to get Biff. He was sitting by the fireplace, still yawning and holding the brandy bottle.

"Lay off that stuff," I told him. "Boss wants to talk to you. Take off your shoes."

"What? What's wrong with my shoes?"

"One of them's got blood on it."

He pulled off his big clodhoppers and examined them. "What do you know? How'd that happen?"

"Did you check the library when you were skulking around the house?"

"Sure."

"And you walked by a dead body without noticing?"

"Did I? Hell, I couldn't find the light switch."

"It's on the wall."

"Couldn't find it in the dark. So I just walked into the room a ways and came right back out."

"And almost stepped on a dead body and bloodied your shoe."

"I was doped."

"No you weren't, you hadn't had any coffee yet. Come on, Conroy wants to talk to you."

"Jeez, this ain't my lucky day. Do you think my breath stinks?"

"I hope Marge can find you a new job. Let's go."

We walked back to the library and Conroy gave Biff holy hell.

"You been drinking, officer?" he asked, after he'd laid into Biff about stepping into puddles of blood and not noticing corpses.

"Just trying to wake up, sir. Me and Hatchett here got doped."

"That's true," I said. "Somebody, the killer likely, drugged our coffee."

"Hell of a place this is," said Conroy. "Go back out, both of you, and make sure everybody's in the living room. Great room. Whatever. I'll be out in a couple of minutes to question them."

14

When we got to the great room, folks were milling around. When I told them Conroy would be in to question them, they looked daggers at me. More questioning? I was afraid the homicide dick might be the second murder victim in one night.

I noticed Bosco and Mavis were sitting well apart. Bosco came up to me, screwed his face into a sappy smile, and opened his mouth.

"No jokes," I told him. "I'm in no mood for crying."

"I was just going to say this place makes me wish I was back in the circus."

"How's your boss? How's Dunty?"

"Fit as a fiddle and ready for love. Go talk to him."

I found him on his favorite love seat, next to Cleo. Mary Elizabeth was standing in front of them.

"Mr. Dunty," she was saying, "our knitting lessons will continue just like before. But not until after all this is over. I can't concentrate."

"There, there," soothed Cleo, "of course you can't concentrate. A delicate girl like you isn't made to endure killings in the household."

"Poor Mr. Cotton. I just can't believe it."

I turned to Dunty. "You holding up OK? How's the heart?"

"I'm surviving, Mr. Hatchett. But I don't know how much more of this my heart can take."

"Buck up, Mr. Flinders," I said. "Buck up The whole ordeal will be over soon. Say, where's Cam?"

"Isn't he here?" Dunty looked around. "Why, he's missing. Find Mayhew and have him call down and tell Cam to come at once."

I went off to find Mayhew. He was sitting with Abigail, and they both looked old and tired.

"Mr. Dunty would like you to summon Cam."

"I'd completely forgotten. How careless of me. I'll call him at once."

"And tell him to bring his wife. It's time she became part of our happy little family."

"His wife, sir? Cam hasn't any — "

"He's got a wife all right. Tell Cam to bring her and don't take no for an answer."

I drifted over to where Simone was standing. "Handling things OK, Simone?"

"As much as can be expected. Is there a lot of blood in the library?"

"About a quart."

"How tragic. Blood stains are so hard to get out,

and it's a genuine Persian carpet, sir."

"Don't let it get you down."

I found Mavis. She was frowning. "Ready for more questions?"

"No. And they'll be the same questions, won't they? Why doesn't anybody take notes? I'm thinking of giving notice."

"Don't do that. Things are looking up."

About this time Conroy showed up. The photographer and the coroner had already left, and the word was that a fingerprint expert was coming around. I wondered where he'd been all this time. Maybe stuck in some snow.

"Everybody here?" Conroy asked the Flinders.

"Except for our chauffer, Cam. He'll be here directly."

"With his wife," I said.

Dunty gave me a startled look. "His wife? Who told you he had a wife?"

"Word gets around."

Cleo gawked. "Cam, with a wife? Why haven't I heard about this?"

"You'll be meeting her soon enough," I told her.

"Mr. Flinders," said Conroy, talking over everybody. "Is there someplace private where I can talk to these people?"

"One by one, or all together?"

"One by one, until we've identified the murderer."

"My office will do. Mayhew will show you."

The butler's shoulders were slumping as he led

the homicide dick to Flinders' office. Mayhew needed to go to bed. In fact, we all did.

Biff and the other two uniformed cops were standing around like they dared anyone to make a break for it. Probably all of us wanted to. I sidled over to him. "What do you think, Biff?"

"Me? About what? What's this wife of the chauffeur's look like? Something nice?"

"Nice to know you have a one-track mind."

Conroy still had his first victim in Dunty's office when the fingerprint guy arrived. Conroy came out and showed the guy the library. After he was through dusting in there we took him upstairs to where the knife was still sticking in the wall next to Dunty's bedroom doorframe. The guy dusted the knife, then pulled it free so we could take a look at the note.

It was different from last night's, and from the ones Dunty had received in the mail. It wasn't made up of letters cut from a magazine. It was hand written in crude printing, like the writer was trying very hard to disguise his handwriting. The note said: "Your pretty gray-haired boy is dead. The gray toupee will be your bane. You're next, Dunty Flinders. Prepare to die."

Pretty dramatic. I didn't know if it was a good idea to show the note to Dunty, but who listens to me? Conroy showed it to him and Dunty turned a nice pale lavender. He asked for his pills, his pipe, and his brandy.

Conroy demanded a writing sample from everyone. Mayhew found paper and enough pencils and all the servants and Ursula did their penmanship homework like good boys and girls, then lined up to be fingerprinted. It was quite the assembly line. Everyone looked cranky and tired and they stared crossly at their inky fingertips.

Then Cam showed up with his — brother? The guy sure looked like Cam, but a couple of years younger. Cam caught my eye. "I told you it wasn't what you thought. Whoever told you I was hiding a wife was blowing smoke."

For once I was speechless. Cam and his brother headed over to talk to the Flinders. Dunty had apparently known about the brother, but I'd made him expect a wife as well. He looked relieved. Cleo looked almost disappointed.

"What happened to your wife, Cam?" she asked him.

"There's no wife, Mrs. Cleo, that's just a rumor. This here's my brother, Cal. He hit town a while back after losing his job back east in Maine. He worked on lobster boats. There's not a lot of those kinds of jobs in Quartz Quarry, so I been letting him stay with me for free. He's been helping me out some. I didn't know if you'd be OK with that or not, but I was getting ready to tell you all about Cal. It's just that I've been kind of busy. You know?"

"So you've been harboring a kinsman in the carriage house without the knowledge of your employers? What do you suppose Mr. Flinders and I should do about that?"

Cam squirmed like a night crawler on a cold fish hook. "Like I said, Mrs. Cleo. I been going to tell you. You know, Cal's done a lot of work around here, even if you didn't know it, and all for free."

"You're very naughty, Cam. Mr. Flinders and I will have to discuss this matter."

"Yes, ma'am."

I caught Dunty making faces, and realized that he was tipping Cam a secret wink. Everything was going to be just fine.

I was listening to this conversation but keeping my eyes on the folks providing samples of their handwriting. I'm not completely useless. I'd noticed one or two things during my time in the Flinders' house. One was that Mavis was left handed. But as she wrote a copy of the threatening note for Conroy to inspect, she used her right hand. Why would she do that if she hadn't written the original note? Interesting. She hadn't been able to sidestep the fingerprinting process though.

Conroy went through his interviews in pretty good time. When he was done he gathered up his boys and left. Cleo tried to get him to leave another officer, but Conroy was having none of it.

"I need my cops on their beats. We've already given you Officer Munson, and that's all we can do for you. Get that detective of yours working harder. He can break the case. He's done it before."

I didn't know if I should thank him or boot him in the pants. But he was right. I hadn't been doing my job. I'd been watching the household for three days and I had nothing. Paddy Cotton had been my main suspect, and he was dead. I had some other ideas, but none I was in love with. I needed to talk to Biff. We were both still tired from whatever sleeping drug we'd been doped with, but Mayhew had brought us more coffee, assuring us that he had watched the process from beginning to end, and had even consumed a cup himself to make sure the brew was undoctored.

While we were drinking it, the ambulance finally showed up and carted away what remained of Paddy Cotton. The snow was screwing everybody up. I took Biff aside and told him I needed to talk to him.

"Hey, can it wait? I'm still woozy."

"Yeah? From the doped coffee you drank, or all the brandy you had?"

"I only had a couple of sips, honest."

"I'd like some shuteye myself, but I've got to get a handle on this case. Come on, let's go someplace where we can talk. Let's go to the library."

"Why there? We'll just talk out here."

"What's the matter, you afraid of blood?"

"Not if it ain't my own. But still — "

"Come on, you chump. You can keep your eyes closed."

I dragged him into the library and closed the door. The room smelled of gore, and the big stain of blood on the swell Persian rug was crusting over. It helped me think.

"Listen, Biff, before I found Paddy's body I was pretty sure he was the guy behind this murder-threat business."

"Guess you was wrong, huh?"

"Maybe not."

"How's that? He's just pretending to be murdered?"

"No, but I think someone may have killed him because they were trying to save Dunty."

"You mean somebody figured out Paddy was the would-be killer and they bumped off Paddy to save the old man's life?"

"That's it."

"Why not just call in the coppers?"

"I think there was a blackmail angle. Paddy had the goods on whoever found him out and he tried to make a deal."

"I don't know, I think you're blowing smoke, Hatchett."

"Speaking of which, how's about we torch a couple of Cuban cigars?" I went over and found the humidor and plucked out a pair of brown beauties. While we were puffing on them I told Biff my ideas. "I think Mavis might have a little cinnamon roll in the oven."

"That right? Yours?"

"My guess is the proud father is Bosco. The Flinders don't approve of that kind of thing. If Mavis doesn't find a dark alley butcher to help her with the situation, she'll start showing pretty soon. That'll be the end of her job. And if the Flinders figure out Bosco's the father, then his job's gone too. That's not a good spot to be in when you're starting a family. If Paddy had the situation figured out he might have threatened to expose Mavis and Bosco if they didn't cooperate with him. Get it?"

"Sure, but you're forgetting something."

"What's that?"

"The killer made another move tonight. What about that dagger with the note on it? And that damned screaming. It's still ringing in my ears."

"Think about it. If they killed Paddy, they'd want to hide their crime by getting somebody else blamed for it. Why not take over where Paddy left off? They must have felt Dunty's heart was stronger than rumored."

"Sure, I see. But it still don't work."

"Quit being smart. I had you pegged for a dumb cop."

"Who, me?"

"Look, the note was hand written. Why? Because it was a different note from the one Paddy had ready. They needed to make his death look like part of the plan to scare old Flinders to death. They didn't have time to play paper dolls with magazines.

"But what about that scream? It was the same as the one I heard the night before. There can't be two people on earth who can make that sound.

Hell, maybe the person who was helping Paddy agreed to help whoever killed him. Something like that. Maybe the screamer's the one that threw that spear."

"So, who knows how to throw spears around here?"

"I don't know, but I think I know who wrote the note. Mavis. When she was preparing her sample of her handwriting, she used her right hand. I'm pretty certain she's left-handed. And I think she might know how to use a bow and arrow, so maybe she knows a little about spear chucking. In fact, she told me herself that she was a track and field star in high school. She might have learned to throw the javelin. Bosco worked in the circus at one time. Circus performers learn all kinds of crazy things. Abigail's taught all the girls around here how to throw knives. Any one of the female servants could be in on this killing."

"Naw, not that sweet little twist, Mary Elizabeth. Corn pone wouldn't melt in her mouth. She wouldn't hurt a fly."

"No? How many chickens' heads did she chop off with an axe on that farm she grew up on?"

"Chickens ain't people."

"Granted, but don't assume that Mary Elizabeth is incapable of violence."

"If you say so. But what could Paddy have had on her that he could use for blackmail?"

"Always shooting down my ideas, aren't you? How's this: Paddy was sleeping with Mary Elizabeth. What if he threatened to tell Cleo? She'd drop the girl like a hot Gila monster. And here's another thing. Dunty and Mary Elizabeth have been sneaking off so she could give him knitting lessons. How hard would it be for Paddy to make Cleo believe that her aged husband was getting a little on the side from her favorite maid?"

"You've got a filthy mind."

"It sometimes takes a filthy mind to be a good detective. Are you saying you're better than me?"

"Maybe. Say, weren't you kind of disappointed when the chauffeur's wife turned out to be the chauffeur's brother instead? I was getting all ready to meet a new dame."

"I don't know how Marge puts up with you. All I know about this case is that there's two would-be murderers working together. Now that the phones are working again, I'm going to make a few calls. I just hope that the Flinders still have the numbers for their servants' references."

"There's an idea. See, now you're using your head. Hey, is that brandy over there?"

15

It was three in the morning. When Biff and I got back to the great room no one was there except Bosco and Ursula. The jester was massaging the girl's shoulders while she cried. It wouldn't take her long to replace Paddy, but maybe she had actually liked the guy.

"You two should go back to your rooms, now that all the excitement's over," I said.

Ursula let out a sob with a lot of volume to it. She'd been wearing makeup, despite having come straight from bed, and a thin wrapper barely covered a thinner night gown.

"I'm going back to bed," I told them, trying to lead by example. "So's Officer Munson, once he's drained his brandy glass. I'll see everybody at breakfast."

"Let's hope we're all still alive by then," said Bosco. I didn't think he was joking.

Biff and I walked to our rooms and a few minutes later at least one of us was asleep. Me.

Nothing like a bloody murder to put a guy to sleep. I wondered if Mayhew would give me a wakeup call, but I needn't have worried. At six-thirty there was a weary knock at my door. I opened up. Mayhew's tie was crooked and his bald head had a grayish hue.

"Tough night," I said.

"Definitely, sir. What has become of the Flinders' household? Murder and mayhem. I'm afraid, sir, breakfast may be a bit delayed this morning. None of us are entirely perky."

"Understandable. Don't worry about it. I just wish I could figure things out and wrap up this case. I'm not ready for another night like the last three."

"I'm sure you're doing your best, sir."

"No, I'm not. Nothing's clear to me at all. Did you know I actually thought Paddy was the guy behind all this gray toupee business? Shows how much I know, doesn't it? Thanks for the wakeup call. Did you wake Officer Munson?"

"Yes, sir. He was sleeping very soundly."

"Good for him. I may need his assistance to-day."

I got up and dressed in the same cotton pants and shirt I'd worn the day before. I went down the hall to the bathroom and used it long enough to shave and plaster down my hair. When I got to the dining room people were still straggling in. Dunty and Cleo were there, sitting side by side for a change. Biff was there, sitting next to Dirk. They were ignoring each other. Biff looked happy as a clam, but Dirk looked like he'd lost a pint of blood during the night. I wondered what was up.

The food was late in getting to the table and, for once, Abigail had failed to turn out a perfect meal. Some of the toast was burned and the scrambled eggs were overcooked and the bacon was flabby.

Nobody complained. Dunty, Cleo, and Ursula were wearing black. Bosco didn't tell one joke. Mavis and Mary Elizabeth waited on us like they had lead weights in their sensible shoes. All and all not a great way to start the day. When the maids were out of the room for a moment I asked Dunty if he'd kept the phone numbers for the people who'd provided references for the servants.

"Perhaps," he said. "In the files in my office. Why?"

"I need more information if I'm going to crack this case. I'd like to call the folks who referred the help, see if they can answer some questions for me."

"Do you still insist the criminal is not an outsider?"

"Absolutely. You don't have to agree with me."

"You're nuts, shamus," Dirk put in his oar for no particular reason.

"He ain't nuts," Biff said in my defense. "I agree with him. This is an inside job if ever there was one."

"I'll provide the references for you," Dunty

promised. "First thing after breakfast."

"That'll be swell. I'll need a phone. Can I use the one in your office?"

"Yes, of course."

After we ate I took Biff to one side and said: "I need your help. I can't call anybody for a reference concerning Ursula. Do you think you can talk to her, in a friendly way, and try to pump her for some information? Just get her background if you can."

"Sure. I don't mind doing that."

"Do you think you can keep your tongue from lapping your shoes while you're talking to her? Think of Marge."

"I was right last night. You got a filthy mind."

"Good luck with Ursula. Don't let her dumb act fool you, and don't let her charm you."

"I got things under control, don't worry."

I found Dunty and he took me into his office and fussed over a filing cabinet for about ten minutes before coming up with a bunch of typed sheets of paper. They had the servants' names on them and a list of references.

"Some of these people may not even be alive," he told me. "We've been blessed with our help. There hasn't been much turnover."

"I'm not going to bother with Mayhew and Abigail."

"Good. Cam and Bosco don't have references."

"Why is that? Did you just hire them out of the blue?"

"In a way, yes. Cam showed up one day looking for work. He said he had experience as a yardman and gardener and was handy with odd jobs. Our caretaker had recently moved to a different state to take care of an aged parent and so Cam's appearance was fortuitous. Later, when our chauffeur was killed in a horrible car accident, Cam took over his duties as well.

"Bosco also showed up on our doorstep unsolicited. He said he was a friend of Cam's. An unusual friendship I'd say. Bosco was so eager to work that we decided to give him a try. He wasn't particularly gifted as an under butler, but he was always telling jokes and stories, and Cleo took a shine to him. The rest you know."

"OK. So that leaves Simone, Mavis, and Mary Elizabeth whose references I can check. It's something, anyway."

"Good luck. I'll leave you to your telephoning."

I started with Simone Brisket, housekeeper. She had been referred by a Mr. and Mrs. Buster Sandhill. When I called I identified myself as the personal secretary for a young couple with very active twelve-year-old twin boys. I had to run the gauntlet through three servants before I finally got to speak with Mrs. Sandhill. She was cool and unhelpful and she didn't like some of my questions. I persevered.

"Listen, Mrs. Sandhill, just between you and me, the twins are a real handful. Their parents, especially their dad, wants the boys to grow up in a manly fashion. Lots of sports and supervised roughhousing. We're thinking of hiring Simone, and we don't want to frighten her away with the wrong questions. Do you happen to know if she can throw a boomerang? Can she box? How is she with the javelin throw? Does she know any wild animal calls? Is archery on her list of accomplishments? Is she much of a fisherman, or fisherwoman?"

"Young man, are you serious?"

"Absolutely."

"I think you've picked the wrong person as housekeeper. Simone was very professional when she was with us. Her private life was of course her own. I haven't any idea if she is athletic, but I'm pretty certain she is not a pugilist and is not well acquainted with the boomerang. Good day."

Hoity-toity. I called the folks who had referred Mavis next. A Mr. Ramsey Smink. Mr. Smink was unfortunately no longer alive. He had died in a messy polo accident, back East, only days before my call. I was politely asked to leave his survivors in peace. I was striking out big. Mary Elizabeth's reference turned out to be her mother. I called her at the farm. After many rings the phone was answered by a breathless woman who sounded about the right age to be Mary Elizabeth's mom.

"Hello?"

"Mrs. Crump?"

"Yes?"

"My name is Clive Hocksworth, personal secretary to the Path-Happintons. I'm calling in regard to your daughter, Mary Elizabeth. We're considering hiring her as a maid, but we have a few questions we'd rather not bother her with. The Path-Happintons have twin boys of an active and inquisitive nature. Tell me, Mrs. Crump, is Mary Elizabeth a physically active girl? She appears a bit frail and wan to me."

"No, sir. Mary Elizabeth grew up on the farm here. She's a sturdy, hard-working girl. Did something happen to her spot at the Flinders?"

"Not exactly, but the household is in a shambles right now. Do you happen to know if Mary Elizabeth can shoot a bow and arrow?"

"I'm sure she could if she wanted to."

"But you didn't teach her?"

"No, sir, that's not very handy on a farm."

"What about spear throwing? Did she spear fish around your place any?"

"I'm sure she could."

"But you didn't teach her?"

"No, but her brothers taught her all kinds of things."

"They taught her to throw a spear?"

"No, not exactly. But her and her brothers used to see who could throw a pitchfork at a hay bale the best. Mary Elizabeth always won."

"Excellent. Boxing?"

"Like I told you, she's got brothers. Knocked out one of Luke's baby teeth in a tussle once."

"Excellent. Is she good at birdcalls, or animal

calls?"

"Don't know. But I do know the hogs sure came when she called. Acted like they was pets."

"Here's my last question. Does Mary Elizabeth have any kind of criminal background?"

"Young man, my barn roof fell in two days ago. I don't have time for this tomfoolery." She hung up.

I grabbed the phone book and made another call. I dialed the number for Top Hatters. I'd been in there once to look at fedoras, but they'd been out of my price range, which I admit is pretty cheap. While I was in there I'd noticed an alcove, dimly-lit, off the main sales room, where there was a display of men's' wigs. A very chipper-sounding fellow answered the phone.

"Top Hatters, finest hats in town. When it's on your head you'll have a smile on your face."

"Yes. I have a kind of an embarrassing question to ask."

"Is it about men's hair pieces, sir?"

"As a matter of fact, yes. Can I ask for your discretion?'

"Absolutely, sir."

"Well, an uncle of mine, who until recently was quite bald, is now all decked out in a new rug. I mean, toupee."

"Yes, sir."

"It looks like some furry animal that was run over but not quite killed. I don't know how to tell him. What I'd like to do is buy him a new one.

You know, make him a little present."

"Very kind of you ,sir. I'm certain we can help you."

"Well, he's an elderly man. He bought a gray toupee. Would you happen to have any of those?"

"Oh, yes, sir. Gray, white, whatever you need."

"I'd hate to think you sold him the one he's wearing, but he's kind of a cheap skate. Maybe he bought some sale item of yours. Have you sold any seedy-looking rugs lately?"

"Oh, that wig, sir. Believe me, we didn't want to. We carry a fine line of quality — but reasonably priced — hairpieces. However, this particular customer was looking for something quite inexpensive. Cheap, actually. The customer was actually a woman, maybe forty, wanting to buy a hairpiece for her uncle, I believe she said. We ordered one from an overseas distributer. It was a truly awful toupee. It was made from badger-bristle"

"Sounds like the customer was one of my cousins. Could you describe her?"

"Well, I saw her a few times. She wouldn't give us a phone number where we could reach her when the toupee arrived. She kept stopping by to check on it. Paid cash, too. She was around middle height, slender, with a full head of wavy black hair. Heavily made up. Dressed in rather old-fashioned clothes. She wore glasses. I didn't observe the color of her eyes. She said her name was — let me see — Mary Ann something."

"Well, my uncle was likely too embarrassed to

make the purchase himself. Probably my cousin Mary Ann did the shopping for him. When would this have been?"

"The wig arrived a few days ago. Excuse me, sir, why all the questions? Is there something you're not telling me?"

"No. I'm kind of a busy-body. Listen, I'll probably be in to see you pretty soon. Thanks for your help."

I hung up and made another call. This one I was looking forward to. The phone rang twice.

"Hello?" a loud, unpleasant, voice said.

"Tracy?"

"Axe! Is that you, my little pickled cucumber?"

"Jeeze! I finally got ahold of you. How you holding up?'

"Not so good without you. Are you still at the mansion?"

"Yes, but not for long. I hope to wrap up the case today. Maybe I can see you this evening. Tomorrow at the latest. Tell me you didn't get frostbite from all this snow."

"Not even close. I've hardly stepped out the door. Cookie scooped the sidewalk. You aren't making eyes at any cute maids, are you?"

"Naw. There aren't any good-looking dames around here. And if there were it wouldn't matter. I've only been thinking of you. Listen, I've really been missing Rocko's food."

"I don't think anybody's ever said that before. Are they starving you there?"

"Not even close. I've probably gained five pounds. You still wearing my ring?"

"Of course. I wouldn't take it off if I was dead."

"Say something insulting so I know it's really you."

"Can't think of anything. Maybe when I see you in the flesh. Make it soon, will you?"

"Quick as I can."

We said some other things that are kind of private and I hung up.

16

I headed to the great room. The hulking Dirk was there, a cigarette sticking out of his face. He was playing solitaire with a deck of cards at a small table near the fireplace. Biff was sitting at the same table. He was also playing solitaire. These guys must really hate each other if they couldn't even engage in a friendly game of poker.

Dunty, Cleo, Bosco and Ursula were also in the great room, but they were just sitting. Nobody was talking. Bosco wasn't regaling the crowd with any stale jokes. I grabbed Biff and coaxed him into a quiet corner.

"Yeah, what do you want?" he whispered.

"You know what I want. How'd it go with Ursula?"

"She ain't such a cold fish. I was surprised. But she ain't your murderer. Too much a scaredy-cat. She's been a secretary for more than ten years. Last job she had she worked for a guy that came on to her. Know what I mean? He took her skiing with him one weekend last winter and that's where she met Paddy Cotton. She's been with him ever since. She won't say one bad word about him. Starts crying every time you mention his name. Sorry I couldn't get nothing better out of her. Like maybe she likes killing babies or something."

"That's all right. I didn't really suspect her of anything anyway. I just needed to make sure. You did fine."

"Can I have a raise and a promotion?"

"Sure. And a company car and your own corner office. When's lunch, I wonder. Think it will be on time?"

"You know the house better than I do. I ain't seen many servants this morning. Pretty shook up I guess."

"Who isn't? Listen, I think I've got things figured out."

"Yeah? Fill me in."

"No, I'm still thinking. Maybe I'll spring it on everyone at lunch."

"That ought to kill their appetites."

Biff and I went to our beds. Once in my room I didn't bother with Waldrous's pajamas. I climbed into bed wearing just his silk boxers. Before I could more than shut my eyes I could hear Officer Munson snoring. If there'd been a fire in his fireplace he would have blown it out.

Mayhew woke us for lunch. It was not going to be a happy meal for some people. I had things figured out. I thought I'd dress for the occasion. I picked out a black monkey suit, black shirt, black tie, black shoes. I should have dyed my brown hair and mustache black.

We assembled as usual in the dining room. The meal was marginally better than breakfast, and the service was better, too. Even Dirk was looking better, but you can't have everything. I was glad Biff was with us; I'd have someone to turn the murderer over to. I let everybody eat before I laid into them. I also asked Mavis and Mary Elizabeth to stay and enjoy my little speech.

"Here's how things shake out," I told everyone.

"Did you hear about the roofer who got the shakes when he was shingling?" asked Bosco, but his heart wasn't in it.

"Paddy Cotton's your man," I said. "He was the brains behind the gray toupee threats. Oh, not the original ones, the ones concerning Waldrous. Mayhew can tell us a few things about that. The second gray toupee was picked up by a young woman belonging to this household. She disguised herself to look older. The winter weather probably helped. She could wear an overcoat and get by with it. I figure she borrowed one of Cleo's wigs and put on a lot of extra makeup."

"What are you saying?" demanded Cleo. "Surely you can't be accusing one of our girls of being part of a murder plot?"

"No, Mr. Flinders. The murder plot was all on Paddy's side. I figure he told Mary Elizabeth that he was only trying to put a scare into the old man so that he'd have another heart attack. Nothing fatal. Just something that would weaken him so Paddy could talk you into gaining control of the family fortune. Of course, I imagine you brought your own money to the marriage and still control it."

"My little princess? You're insane!"

"Not even close. Paddy seduced her." I heard a gasp from Ursula, but I didn't pause. "Once he'd talked her into sleeping with him he not only had her cooperation but also something to blackmail her with. He made her believe that after you adopted her, which would be certain after Dunty's health was weakened, he would marry her, and everyone would live happily ever after.

"Paddy was the one who shot the arrow at me. He was the one who set the booby trap on the stairs for me. He had the servants' door in his bedroom unblocked so he could more conveniently visit Mary Elizabeth at night while he was still servicing Ursula. No wonder he was aging fast!"

Everyone was motionless and silent. So, I took a breath and kept rolling.

"Mary Elizabeth spiked the carafe of coffee Biff and I drank, and it was her hog-calling talent that allowed her to make those God-awful banshee screams two nights running. She also helped Paddy with the notes and preparations. When they met in the library last night, everyone was asleep, and they figured Biff and I would be knocked-out for hours.

"However, Mavis interrupted them while they were cutting letters out of a magazine and pasting them on a sheet of stationary."

"Mavis!" said Cleo. "What did she have to do with it?"

"She didn't have anything to do with it. It was accidental. You see, Mavis liked to practice her singing in the library when everyone was in bed. The library is practically sound proof with its walls of books and thick carpets. So, why was she practicing her singing? Because she and Bosco are planning on buying a club, someday. Mavis will sing and Bosco will tell jokes."

"Mavis and Bosco? I never!"

"Just listen to me, Mrs. Flinders. Bosco and Mavis are a couple. In fact, they might have a little one on the way. Don't be too harsh with them. In the case of love, these things happen. Maybe they'll marry. Anyhow, Mavis caught Paddy and Mary Elizabeth preparing their most recent installment in the 'Let's Scare Mr. Dunty To Death' campaign.

"Mavis threatened to expose them — of course she did! She likes Mr. Dunty, as well as you, Mrs. Cleo. So Paddy likely tried to bribe her. When that didn't work, he used threats. He said he'd go to you and your husband, tell you that Mavis was pregnant, and reveal Bosco as the father. That would ruin things for them. You'd probably dismiss both of them, and Mr. Dunty would take them out of the trusts. On top of that, when they went looking for new jobs you'd give them bad references. So Mavis agreed to keep quiet, but only if Paddy and Mary Elizabeth would give up their plan.

"When Paddy wouldn't agree, he and Mary Elizabeth probably got into a fight. Maybe Mary Elizabeth thought Mavis was right. Maybe they should stop trying to scare the old man. So, what happens? Paddy threatens Mary Elizabeth. He tells her that if she doesn't continue to cooperate with him he'll go to you, Cleo, and reveal that your little princess has been sleeping with him. And here's the thing. Mary Elizabeth has been giving Mr. Dunty knitting lessons. They spend a little time each day locked up in his office, playing with knitting needles. Isn't that right, Mrs. Flinders?"

"Yes, but what of it?"

"Nothing, except Paddy was likely going to claim to you that your husband and Mary Elizabeth were having a little amour. That would have ruined Mary Elizabeth's reputation. No adoption, no trust money, no job."

I noticed that Mary Elizabeth's cheeks were wet. She was crying, but not making a sound. I continued.

"She got mad at Paddy. But his threats to expose her weren't the worst part. He had exposed himself as a cheap blackmailer and a gigolo who just used women. He was no longer Mary Elizabeth's dreamy knight in shining armor. He was just a cheap crook looking for money."

Mary Elizabeth's shoulders were beginning to shake, and both Dunty and Cleo were looking at her.

"I figure it like this," I told them. "Mavis had brought that Zulu spear to the library with her for protection. Everybody around here has pillaged the trophy room for weapons. She had leaned it up against a table or something. Then Paddy decided to let the girls talk things over while he planted the next note. When he turned his back to them and headed out of the library, that's when Mary Elizabeth — angry, hurt, disappointed — grabbed the spear and flung it at Paddy's retreating back."

"I won't believe it!" said Cleo. "You've gone too far, Mr. Hatchett."

"Your little princess used to have pitchfork throwing contests with her brothers back on the farm. Her aim was pretty good. But maybe she didn't really intend to kill Paddy. She might only have wanted to scare him. But the spear slipped through a couple of ribs and entered Paddy's heart. Judging by the amount of blood on the library floor, Paddy probably lived for a couple of minutes more."

"That's appalling," said Dunty. "But, if Mr. Cotton was the one terrorizing me, then how do you explain the knife and the note, and the awful scream? According to you, he was dead when those things happened."

"Sure, but Mary Elizabeth and Mavis were in a

pickle. They didn't want to be blamed for Paddy's death. So, what did they do? They decided to keep up with the gray toupee plan for a little while longer. Let the mysterious would-be killer take the blame for murdering Paddy. Make it look like part of the killer's plan."

I turned to address Mavis and Mary Elizabeth. "Have I got things about right, girls?"

"I didn't mean to kill him!" wailed Mary Elizabeth. "It just happened, I was so mad, and hurt. He betrayed me. He was horrid. He would have ruined me. I just grabbed up the spear and threw it. I aimed for it to hit the floor at his feet, but I missed. It wasn't like throwing a pitchfork at all."

"I think she's telling the truth," said Mavis. "She screamed horribly when the spear hit him. I'm surprised no one heard it. And what were we to do? It was an accident, and he deserved to be killed after treating us so awful, and wanting to kill Mr. Dunty. I know we should have gone straight to Officer Biff, but we thought he was asleep, and we panicked. I wrote the new note and fastened it to the wall outside Mr. Dunty's room, and Mary Elizabeth gave her hog call scream."

"I'm very disappointed in both of you girls," said Cleo, severely. "Killing Paddy, and trying to hide it. Mary Elizabeth, how could you have granted the final favor to Mr. Paddy? I thought you were a nicer girl than that. And you, Mavis, getting with child by a court jester. I could not have thought it possible. Mary Elizabeth, adoption is now completely out of the question. Mavis, I hope you and Bosco are planning to marry. Think of the child."

"I think that wraps things up, except for Mayhew's story," I said. "If I'm not mistaken, your butler knows something about Waldrous Flinders' death."

"Time to call in more coppers," said Biff, rising from the table. "Let me find a phone."

"That snake," hissed Ursula. "Him and his telling me that I was the only one he ever loved. Telling me he was going to marry me. I've had enough of this place." She left the table, presumably to go to her room.

"What has become of Flinders Manor?" said Dunty. "What has become of our servants, our guests? We must really check our references better next time. Don't you think, dear?"

"Without question," said Cleo.

"Hey, did you hear the one about the stripper who tried to cover up her background?" asked Bosco.

"Shut your mouth, Bosco," said Cleo. "I want no more of your jokes. Go to your room."

"Sure, but I'm taking a rum bottle with me. Can't you forgive me and Mavis? We were going to do the right thing."

"We'll see," said Dunty.

"Anybody got anything to say to me?" I asked. "I cracked the case. That's what you're paying me for."

"And you shall be rewarded well for your service," said Cleo. "And I owe you an apology for not sharing your belief that the would-be killer was right under our roof."

"Forget it," I said. "We all make mistakes. I just wish I'd figured things out faster than I did. Paddy might still be alive."

Biff returned to the dining room. "Cops are on the way. Mary Elizabeth, I'm, going to have to cuff you. Sorry, princess." He took his handcuffs from his belt and put them on her right then. Her whole body was shaking now while she wept.

"Don't do that," complained Biff. "You'll make me feel like a heel." He took the princess out into the entry hall to await her probable arrest. Bosco went to his room. Ursula was already in hers.

"Is it all right if I go on about my duties, Ma'am?" Mavis asked Cleo.

"Yes, by all means. And when you clean my room this morning, do a proper job. You girls have been a bit sloppy of late. I don't know what's got into you."

Mavis walked out. That just left Dirk and the Flinders.

"I don't suppose we need your services any longer, Dirk," said Dunty. "Perhaps you should be on your way. Pack up your things and tell me when you're ready to go. I'll have Mayhew write you a check."

"Just like that, huh?" said Dirk. He got up and left in a huff.

"I want to thank you for what you've done," Dunty told me. "I feel greatly relieved." He pulled a nice handkerchief from his jacket pocket and mopped his brow with it. Then he picked up the bell he used to summon Mayhew and rang it vigorously. I sat down to finish my now-cold coffee.

When Mayhew arrived, still looking a little worse for wear, Dunty said: "Bring my pipe and tobacco, and some brandy. And when you return I want a word with you."

"Yes, sir. Right away, sir. And your pills?"

"Leave them be. I don't believe I need them now. There's something appalling about taking nitroglycerin. Makes a man feel like he's going to blow up at any minute."

"Yes, sir."

When the butler returned, Dunty settled in with his pipe and brandy and told Mayhew to sit down.

"Beg your pardon, sir? Sit down? In your presence, sir?"

"I'm not a king, or a sultan, or some such. Yes, be seated."

Mayhew lowered himself onto the edge of a chair and gave Dunty a hang dog look. "Nothing amiss I hope, sir."

"Mr. Hatchett here says you know something about my brother's death that you have failed to reveal in the past. Is that true, Mayhew?"

The butler sighed. "It's a long story, sir. Shall we arrange for a more convenient time?"

"No. This is quite convenient enough. What have you been hiding from us?"

"I never meant to hide anything, sir. But it was a family matter. I'm afraid, sir, and madam, that my brother killed your brother."

"What?" Dunty actually grabbed his hair and tugged on it. "This whole house has gone mad. I'm going to sell it, move into one of those little trailer houses. Go on."

"Well, sir, to begin. I had a half-brother, Carson, conceived, to use the vernacular, on the incorrect side of the coverlet. He was a good-hearted chap, quite charming and carefree, but a slave to his vices. Drinking, gambling, and," he cleared his throat, "women. He was raised in service, as I was, but he remained in England when I moved here. For a time he worked for Lady Cecily Carstairs. You know the Carstairs, sir?"

"I'm not familiar with them."

"Fine family, sir, and Lady Cecily was the best of the lot. Generous to a fault, though I shouldn't say it. One night, Carson — badly wanting to pay a gambling debt — broke into a manor hard by the Carstairs' residence and was apprehended. However, Lady Cecily used her considerable influence to keep my brother out of the prison system. Despite this, she was not willing to keep him on as her own servant. He was an under butler, sir.

"At about the same time — this was twenty-five years ago — your own brother, Mr. Waldrous, made his determination to see the world, including some of its less savory parts. He needed a manservant. I arranged, through Lady Cecily, to have my brother recommended for the position."

"Certainly, I remember. Waldrous wanted someone who wasn't afraid to knock about a bit, explore the backwaters of the world and not complain about the conditions. This Carson was referred to us by Lady Carstairs. I remember her name now, but I am not acquainted with her family."

"That's how my half-brother became Mr. Waldrous' manservant. He traveled from Devonshire to Quartz Quarry and applied for the position in person. Mr. Waldrous was favorably impressed and hired him on the spot. It was the making of my brother. For years he served Mr. Waldrous faithfully and well. We kept in touch through the post."

"Yes, yes, go on." Dunty pulled again at his hair.

"My brother, like myself, went bald at an early age. Unlike me, he was disturbed by his loss of hair. He considered it unmanly, and began to affect a hairpiece. As the years went by his remaining hair began to turn gray. And so he purchased a fine gray toupee. You have seen that toupee."

"So this Carson was the one who hounded poor Waldrous and, I gather, cut off his head."

"I tried to stop him, sir, I really did. I was in communication with Carson up to the very last. I thought I had him talked out of murdering Mr.

Waldrous. Sadly, I was mistaken."

"Sadly, indeed! What possessed your brother to want to murder mine?"

"A practical joke, sir."

"How could that be?"

"If you'll recall, sir, your brother settled on an estate near Tripoli. He hired a local girl, a native, as upstairs maid. She was quite a fetching young creature from what I gather. Both Carson and Mr. Waldrous became smitten with her."

"Nonsense! My brother smitten with a native girl, a servant?"

"Beauty knows no station, sir. Though she was several years my brother's junior, and could have improved her lot immensely by submitting to Mr. Waldrous' advances, she conceived a regard for Carson that likely would have ended in their marriage, if not for an unfortunate happening."

"The practical joke you spoke of?"

"Yes, sir. I believe it safe to say that Mr. Waldrous was envious of Carson's success with young Dewdrop."

"Silly name."

"The English equivalent of her native name."

"You say my brother was envious? He was incapable of such a low emotion."

"Oh, no, he wasn't," put in Cleo. "He displayed many low emotions. Almost constantly. You don't remember him the way I do, Dunty dear."

"Go on," Dunty said to Mayhew, ignoring his wife.

"One day, when Mr. Waldrous, Carson, and Dewdrop were together, your brother snatched Carson's gray toupee from his head as a joke. The girl was horrified. She didn't mind that Carson was bald, not at all. But she could not accept the fact that he had concealed his baldness from her. She believed that if he could lie to her about such a thing as wearing a hairpiece, then he could deceive her in other ways.

"Dewdrop refused to marry him. Carson was heart-broken. The girl, too, was distraught, and in her extremity of emotion she submitted to Mr. Waldrous' improper romantic advances."

"My brother was not a bounder."

"Yes, he was, Dunty dear," put in Cleo. "I'd call him exactly that, if I were English. A bounder."

I was beginning to think this whole recital was like an old movie, maybe with Rudolph Valentino playing Mayhew's brother. I wanted to say something, but I decided to keep my mouth shut.

"Go on," Dunty said to Mayhew.

"Yes, sir. Dewdrop, having been deflowered by Mr. Waldrous, lost her head and banished herself from the estate. She wandered until she reached the sands of the Sahara and she stepped into a nest of sand vipers. My brother believed she deliberately took her own life."

"Nonsense. She stepped where she shouldn't have, that's all."

It would be vipers, of course. Aren't snakes the root of all evil? Or is it dames...I forget. I kept my opinion to myself.

"My brother became entirely estranged from his master. He left Mr. Waldrous' employment, but before he went, he warned Mr. Waldrous that the day would come when he, Carson, would take the life of the man who had driven his beloved to her death. 'Watch for the gray toupee,' he told him. 'This will be the sign of your impending death.'"

"How many years ago was this?"

"Twenty."

"Your brother went all those years contemplating revenge against Waldrous?"

"Yes. He remained in service for many years, employed by a family that truly appreciated him. However, he finally came down with an especially virulent form of malaria and feared his death was near. He decided he must carry out his threat of vengeance at once, so he traveled back to America, gradually getting closer and closer to Quartz Quarry while sending his letters of threat, and finally the gray toupee itself."

"Why did my brother never tell me of any of this?"

"I suspect he felt he had behaved shabbily, if you'll excuse me for saying so, sir."

"Yes, well and good. But when death was dogging his very heels? Why not come to me then and make a clean breast of things? I might have been able to help him."

"That was my doing, sir. I went to him privately and told him I was in correspondence with Carson and that I thought I could talk him out of his revenge. I fully believed that. And I did not want Carson apprehended. I made Mr. Waldrous promise to say nothing of my brother, or the origin of the gray toupee, to anyone. In return I promised to do everything I could to keep Carson from carrying out his revenge for Dewdrop."

"And you failed. You killed my brother!"

"Now, Dunty dear," said Cleo, "this is Mayhew you're talking about. He wouldn't hurt a fly."

"My brother was not a fly, Cleo. Mayhew, if you had reported Carson to the authorities they could have caught him and kept him from chopping off my brother's head!"

"I don't think so, sir. I don't believe anyone could have caught him. It was my impression he was in touch with no one but me. I received monthly letters in which he would give me a post office box number to write to. Then he would go on to the next town, or state, and write me with a new number.

"I'm sure he lived under an assumed name, was perhaps disguised, and watched each post office very closely before retrieving his mail. I was Mr. Waldrous' only hope, and I wrote to Carson time and time again, telling him not to harm your brother.

"In the end, he wrote and told me that he had given up his idea of vengeance. It was a trick, and I fell for it. I feel terribly guilty because of Mr.

Waldrous' death, but I could not have prevented it by volunteering what little information I had concerning my brother's whereabouts, sir."

As we sat there, I kept expecting a flourish of music to announce the credits at the end of the film. Hell, it could be an opera, not that I have experience with such things.

17

Dunty puffed away on his calabash, then poured out and drank a good stiff jolt of brandy. It appeared to calm him.

"Never mind, Mayhew. Perhaps you're right. But your brother is still at large and I don't like that."

"My brother, sir, is dead."

"Are you certain?"

"Yes, sir. He wrote me a letter on his deathbed. The postmark was Cincinnati. After a few weeks without hearing from him further, I made inquiries. My brother indeed died and was buried in Cincinnati. He left no will and gave what remained of his money to a home for wayward sailors. He always loved the sea."

"So, when I received my first threatening letter, and then that unspeakable toupee, you knew it could not be your brother's work?"

"Indeed, sir, I knew that. It was as much a mystery to me as it was to you."

"Thank God it's over. The whole ordeal."

"Is it, sir?"

"Yes, haven't you heard? I figured the servants would know about it almost at once. Mr. Paddy was the fiend behind the plot to kill me. His helper was Mary Elizabeth, who ended up spearing him to death. Mavis found them out."

"Pray, sir, give me the details!"

"Not now. I'm too upset, too harried. Perhaps Mr. Hatchett can acquaint you with what happened."

"I'd be happy to," I told Mayhew. "Why don't you and me take a little walk, if Mr. and Mrs. Flinders can spare you for a while."

"Yes, of course," said Dunty.

"Walk this way, Mayhew," I said, and led him outside into the cold, sunshiny, day.

"A fine day, sir," said Mayhew.

"Certainly is. I'm looking forward to getting in my car and leaving this joint."

"An understandable sentiment, sir."

"Listen, I'm sorry I put you on the spot in there, but I thought things needed to be cleared up."

"You did what was best for all, sir. To tell the truth, I'm glad I was forced into a confession. It clears the air. I really don't like keeping secrets from Mr. Dunty and Mrs. Cleo."

I gave Mayhew the parts of the story he didn't know. "I hope I didn't get you into too much hot water. You're a swell guy."

"I appreciate that, sir, coming from you."

"Thanks for your help these last few days. You're a good butler. Maybe things will get back to normal now."

"One hopes so, sir. And thank you for all you've done. The ghost of the gray toupee is gone."

"I just wish I'd figured things out sooner. Paddy would still be alive, and Mary Elizabeth wouldn't be facing a prison sentence."

"Not your fault, sir. I don't know how you got to the bottom of things the way you did. You're a fine detective."

"Coming from you, that means something. I hope Mavis won't get jail time. She's an accessory after the fact, but she had nothing to do with the killing. I'd hate to think her baby might be born behind bars."

"Surely that won't happen, sir!"

"I guess I'll head inside and change into my dirty clothes and head on out of here."

"You will be missed. You've added a certain rough originality to our lives."

We went inside and I changed clothes in the bedroom and then went to the great room. Dirk was already gone. Dunty and Cleo were alone.

"This may be an odd request," I told the Flinders, "but I always like to have a souvenir of my cases, whenever possible. I don't suppose I could have that ratty gray toupee Paddy mailed you?"

"With my blessing," Said Dunty. He rang the bell for Mayhew.

When the butler arrived, Dunty said: "Fetch my checkbook, Mayhew, and the gray toupee."

"Very good, sir." Mayhew bowed and left. He returned in a few minutes bearing a big check book and a flat box.

Dunty motioned him over and whispered in his ear. Mayhew took a pen from his jacket pocket and wrote out a check, then he handed me both the check and the box.

"I hope the amount is sufficient," said Dunty.

I looked at the check. Boy, was it sufficient.

"You sure you want to give me this much?"

"You earned it."

"Well, then, thank you. I guess this is good-bye. If you ever need a detective again, give me a call."

I donned my hat and coat and strolled out the front door and walked to my car where I'd parked it on a side street near the mansion. Fortunately, it had survived the storm unscathed, except for some splashed mud and slush. It was a little cranky getting started, but when it warmed up it drove just fine. I thought of heading home, but forget that. I drove over to Rocko's instead. There was a hamburger and a swell girl waiting for me.

It'd been a solid month since I'd bid a fond adieu to the Flinders' household. I was working on another case concerning a stolen pair of pet ostriches, and it looked like the job was going to require some tailing on my part. My crimson Nash is too flashy to use for tailing anybody — I'd be spotted in less than a block — so I decided to switch cars with Tracy for the week. Her old brown Chevy is practically invisible. You could park it in someone's living room and they probably wouldn't notice until they tripped over it. I had Tracy drive over to my place to make the switch. She needed practice driving since it'd been so long since she'd owned a car. I waited for her in the little ersatz log cabin I call home.

While I was waiting, I got a phone call.

"Yeah?" I answered.

"This Axe Hatchett?" a gravelly voice asked.

"That's me."

"You going to be around your place for an hour or so? I got a big trunk to deliver to you."

"I'll be here. What kind of trunk? Is it attached to an elephant?"

"Naw, just some stuff you might want. I'll be over as soon as possible."

"Who is this?"

There was no answer. The party had already hung up.

I went on waiting for Tracy and in a few minutes she showed up. I made her coffee and we exchanged car keys and I told her about the mysterious phone call.

"A trunk?" asked Tracy. "Pirates like those. Maybe somebody's bringing you a pile of jewels and pieces of eight. Are those made of gold?"

"Not the kind anybody'd give me. Aluminum maybe."

I'd hardly finished speaking when a rich, melodious, car horn honked out front. We went out into the yard and there was a classy yellow Rolls Royce parked between my Nash and Tracy's Chevy. It made both our cars look like they belonged in a salvage yard. A guy got out of the driver's seat. He was wearing gray jodhpurs tucked into shiny black boots, a gray double-breasted jacket, and a fancy gray cap. I hardly recognized him. It was Cam.

"Hey, Mr. Hatchett. How's tricks? Want to help me carry this trunk into your house?" He opened the boot of the Rolls and together we hauled a big leather, iron-bound, trunk into my living room. Cam gave me a salute, clicked his heels together, and said he had to run.

"Me and my brother still got firewood to cut up. That snowstorm knocked down enough branches to make a forest," he said.

"Things OK at the Flinders' mansion?"

"Same old same old. We got a new maid to replace Mary Elizabeth. I think she's trouble."

"Tell her to stay away from the trophy room."

Cam climbed into his bus and it purred away like a happy kitten.

"Not exactly a talkative guy, is he?" Tracy said.

"Not Cam. He keeps his lip buttoned. Let's see what's in the trunk."

I lifted the lid and there was a note in impeccable handwriting laying on top of a bunch of folded clothes. I read the note out loud:

Dear Mr. Hatchett,

I have recently made the decision to retire from service, and Abigail has made me the happiest of men by agreeing to give me her hand in marriage. The wedding ceremony will be a quiet one, performed by the justice of the peace, with only two witnesses and no guests. Otherwise, rest assured, your name would be on the guest list.

Someone, I believe it was the stalwart Officer Munson, indicated to me that you were contemplating, to use the vernacular, tying the knot. It is my understanding that the profession of private investigator, in spite of its dangers, is not necessarily a lucrative one. Forgive my presumption, but I thought you might possibly be in need of a fine tuxedo for your future wedding. I am sending you Waldrous' best, including the accoutrements. I have also taken the liberty, please forgive me, of sending along several other outfits that I think you might find useful.

Matters have returned to an even keel here at the Flinders Manor. The only change is the hiring of a new maid, a rather hasty girl, to replace Mary Elizabeth. Mr. Dunty and Mrs. Cleo have retained an expensive lawyer to defend Mary Elizabeth. The defense intends to show that the girl slew Mr. Cotton to spare the life of Mr. Dunty.

As soon as Abigail and I have opened our new bakery, we would like to have you and

*your lady over for tea. Good luck in all your
future endeavors. Don't forget to guard
your back.*

   Yours, with gratitude and affection,
   — Mayhew Thrush

"Who's this Mayhew Thrush guy?" asked Tracy.

"A butler among butlers."

"Listen, do you think that Mary Elizabeth kid will get a light sentence?"

"With her looks and a pricey shyster lawyer? Probably."

"When we're married and settled in our own place, let's have Mayhew and Abigail over for dinner."

"You like that kind of thing?'

"I think I could learn to."

"I hate to ask, but do you even know how to cook?"

"Sure. Cookie taught me everything he knows."

"That must have taken about ten minutes, and you'll have to forget all of it. Start with a clean slate. Learn to thaw ice cubes first, then work up to boiling water. Let's look at the monkey suit."

The tuxedo was at the top of the trunk. It was black silk, with satin lapels and a satin stripe down the sides of the legs. The coat was a claw hammer. There was a stiff shirt as white as a bleached peace dove, the kind of shirt my grandpa would have called "boiled". There were cufflinks, and shirt stud dinguses, all made of gray pearls. There was even one of those silk top hats that fold down flat.

"All I need now is a walking stick," I told Tracy.

"No. You can lean on my arm. What classy duds! Try them on."

"No. I'm already dressed."

"Try them on!"

There's no arguing with Tracy. I went into the bedroom and climbed into the tux. I even put on the black shoes that were shiny enough to use for shaving mirrors. When I came back out, Tracy looked at me like I'd just been elected senator.

"It fits like it was made for you. Except for the pants. You'll have to lose a couple of pounds."

"I'll stop eating at Rocko's. Can I take this outfit off now?"

"Only if you promise to put it back on for our wedding."

"It's a deal. Say, you're going to need a dress of some kind, aren't you?"

"Yeah, I think that's how it works. My folks will spring for it. Dad would want me to wear something made out of fringed buckskin, and he'd want it to be cheap. I'll go shopping with Mom. She'll take care of me. So, let's set a date."

"Let's not. I'm not quite ready."

"No? You still thinking about some chamber maid you met at the Flinders'?"

"I don't even remember what the maids looked like. When we do get married, where do you want to go on our honeymoon? Niagara Falls?"

"Nobody goes there. It's too wet and noisy. How about a dude ranch?"

"You're kidding. I don't want to spend my honeymoon on a horse."

"Why not — you scared?"

"I'm not scared of anything. Not even you. At least, not sometimes."

"Think of the sunshine, the beans, the galloping mustangs and cowboy songs."

"What if I fall off my cayuse and break my caboose?"

"Don't worry, we won't shoot you. I'll even buy you that walking stick you want."

END

If you have enjoyed this book, please go to its Amazon book page and leave a short review. It will be most appreciated!

OTHER BOOKS BY THIS AUTHOR:

DEAD MAN LIMPING
[ISBN: 978-1-940469-00-3]

When 1950s private eye Axel Hatchett is hired by a delectable redhead to turn up her missing husband, Hatchett discovers that the man is not only still alive, but is armed, probably crazy, and is on a killing spree that may include Hatchett! But something stinks about this case — big time — and it's not Hatchett's pet skunk, Ambrosia.

GLIMMER IN A GLASS EYE
[ISBN: 978-1-940469-02-7]

After 1950s gumshoe Axel Hatchett is hired to protect a used car dealer from a threat of murder, Hatchett finds himself in a nest of rattlesnakes — literally! When the car dealer is bumped off, and Hatchett's prime suspect is murdered, the sleuth is forced to sift through a deck of also-ran suspects to solve the two killings before another corpse is added. And to make matters worse, he's falling for a mouthy waitress who works in a sleazy diner....

THREE CURSING BIRDS
[ISBN: 978-1-940469-03-4]

When thieves snatch a statue of the bird-headed Egyptian god, Thoth, and drop its owner from a third-story window, 1950s private detective Axel Hatchett is set on their trail. But wait! – there are actually three statues, and one of them may contain a treasure map! Hatchett enlists the aid of his hash-slinging fiancée and a snake-handling English professor to help solve the case of the three cursed birds.

KILLER BEAR FOR HIRE
[ISBN: 978-1-940469-04-1]

In all his years of sleuthing, snarky 1950s private eye Axel Hatchett has never faced a case like this: a bear trained to kill. Hatchett finds himself hunted by a deadly two-legged predator whose bullet comes unnervingly close to Hatchett's new wife, and that has Hatchett seeing red! Armed with a revolver and his caustic wits, Hatchett is out to solve a grizzly killing, or die trying.

BOOK CLUB DISCUSSION QUESTIONS

(To be enjoyed at a multi-course dinner, served by the butler.)

1. Do you feel you fully entered the world of this book? Do you want to stay? (Or maybe it's just a butler we all long for....)

2. Do any of the characters remind you of the irritating court jester in your life?

3. Was the plot engaging—did the story interest you? Do you hope to see the movie version?

4. Was there a transformative moment that changed the hero? Yes? I must have slept through that part.

5. Did you find the book funny? Witty? Droll? Better than Grandpa Ben's endless stories at the dinner table?

6. Was there a moment of epiphany for you when you realized you were missing your favorite re-runs on TV?

7. Did this book remind you of Downton Abbey? Should we exchange scone recipes? What is your favorite tea?

8. Do the characters react the way you think you would in a similar situation? Or would you have grabbed an ancient Viking axe and chopped them all to bits? Over tea?

9. Would you buy another novel by this author? Be prepared to explain yourself if you answered "no" to this question.

10. Do you know where I can purchase a toupee for my pet skunk?

ABOUT THE AUTHOR

Steven LeRoy Nelson is an award-winning humorist whose short fiction has appeared in *Alfred Hitchcock Mystery Magazine*, *Ellery Queen Mystery Magazine*, *The Leviathan*, and numerous other publications.

Visit him at his website at:

www.stevenleroynelson.com